The Desert Lord's Bride

OLIVIA GATES

Olivia Gates has always pursued many passions. But the time came when she had to set up a 'passion priority', to give her top one her all, and writing won. Hands down. She is most fulfilled when she is creating worlds and conflicts for her characters and then exploring and untangling them bit by bit, sharing her protagonists' every heartache and hope and heart-pounding doubt until she leads them to their indisputably earned and glorious happy ending. When she's not writing she is a doctor, a wife to her own alpha male, and a mother to one brilliant girl and one demanding angora cat.

Please visit Olivia at http://www.oliviagates.com

To my wonderful mother, husband and daughter, for the support, enthusiasm and inspiration.

To my amazing editor Natashya Wilson, for always getting the best book out of me.

Can't do it all without you.

Prologue

It was happening.

And Shehab ben Hareth ben Essam Ed-Deen Aal Masood could still barely believe it.

Ya Ullah. Was he really standing in the middle of the ceremonial hall of the citadel of Bayt el Hekmah—which had witnessed every major royal event for six hundred years from the joyous to the grim—draped in the ceremonial garb he'd never thought he'd ever wear, the black-on-black robes of succession?

Yes. He was really here. So was every member of Judar's Tribune of Elders, every member of the royal family, every noble house representative, every gaze focused on him.

He blocked out all but his older brother, Farooq, standing right there in his own ceremonial robes, white on white, signifying the transfer of power, his golden eyes flashing his regret, asking understanding.

Shehab squeezed his eyes shut once, acknowledging, everything once again explained and sanctioned through the elemental bond that had bound them since Shehab was born.

Yes. Shehab understood. And accepted. Farooq was only doing this because he had to. Because he knew Shehab was capable of shouldering the burden.

Then Farooq spoke, his voice reverberating in the gigantic hall, fathomless in tone, final in intent. *"O'waleek badallan menni."*

I bequeath you the succession in my stead.

Then their uncle, the king, barely upright on the throne with the toll of crises, both physical and political, made the intent a reality, in a voice ravaged by infirmity and deep worry.

"Wa ana ossaddek ala tanseebuk walley aahdi."

And I validate naming you my heir.

Shehab went down on one knee in front of his older brother, extending both hands, palms up, to accept the bejeweled sword of succession. The moment the heavy weapon rested on his upturned hands, it felt as if he'd just taken the weight of the world there.

And he had. He'd taken on the weight of Judar's future.

He closed his eyes as the cold steel singed his flesh.

Ya Ullah. It was real.

Days ago he'd been going about his multi-billion-dollar IT business, his contribution to his kingdom being to ensure its avant-garde position in the global technological race. Days ago the throne had been a nonexistent specter with an older heir in his prime preceding him in line to it.

Then came today. Came now.

In place of the freedom to lead his own life, there loomed in his future undreamed-of power. And unspeakable responsibility. All it had taken was ten words.

And now he was Judar's crown prince. Judar's future king.

If there remained a Judar to be future king of. If there remained a throne for him to sit on.

Neither was certain any longer.

Not if he didn't fulfill the terms of the pact demanded by the Aal Shalaans, the second-most powerful tribe of Judar, who formed Judor's most influential minority.

Not if he didn't marry a woman he'd never laid eyes on.

One

Hot as hell, cold as the grave.

Shehab's lips thinned as he recalled the catchphrase, his eyes slicing through the sea of costumed people who impinged on his senses and turned the ballroom into a battleground of material excess and self-serving agendas.

Still no sign of the woman who'd warranted this slogan.

He played it again in his mind, unwillingly finding the rhythm to it, humming it along with the exuberant live orchestral performance of Mozart's Piano Concerto No. 9.

Hot as hell, cold as the grave.

One man had even added *insatiable as death.*

Now *that* was a summation if he'd ever heard one.

The descriptions sounded like titles. Like the ones he'd been saddled with since birth. Sheikh Aal Masood. His Royal Highness. And now His Majestic Eminence the Crown Prince.

But according to common consensus, hers had been earned.

And he was expected to marry the woman.

No. He wasn't expected to. He was going to. He *had* to.

His every muscle clenched. His teeth grated against each other. *Ya Ullah.* He should be resigned by now, numbed. It had been over a month since he'd known the fate he had to succumb to, to safeguard Judar's throne.

At times he could almost hate Carmen.

It was because of Farooq's overriding love for his wife that he'd thrown the burden in Shehab's lap.

Still, Shehab could have endured a fate he'd always proclaimed worse than death, an arranged marriage, if the designated bride had been anyone acceptable.

But Farah Beaumont, the illegitimate daughter of King Atef Aal Shalaan, king of Zohayd, wasn't acceptable.

Not because she'd been born out of wedlock. And not because she'd refused to acknowledge her heritage, or to be the instrument of peace. The first she had no hand in, the second could have been a temporary inability to deal with the revelations about her past, the upheavals it promised in her future.

But neither was why Farah Beaumont—whom her mother had so sneakily given an Arabic name popular in the West—spurned her father and could afford to turn down the prospect of becoming a princess. The real reason was what made her so repulsive.

She'd been born into privilege, having been adopted by the French multimillionaire her mother had married. Then, ever since his fortune had been lost after his death, Farah had been clawing her way back to the top. She'd reached it when she'd become the right hand and mistress of world-shaper Bill Hanson, a married man almost old enough to be her grandfather.

By evidence of her actions and by everyone's testimony, Farah Beaumont was a cold, promiscuous, seriously twisted woman.

She was also crucial to a whole region's peace. But she'd refused to do her duty. Point-blank.

Now he had *his* duty. To pulverize her refusal.

He forced his teeth apart, answered the infringing stare of a couple in Marie Antoinette and Louis XVI costumes.

Instead of deflecting attention by making an appearance as a *Kel Tagelmust,* a man of the veil, a *Tuareg* Sahara warrior, Shehab was attracting nothing but. At least he remained anonymous. He couldn't risk recognition. Hence the masked ball, where he could take the masked part literally.

He exhaled, venting some tension, his breath scorching as it spread behind the indigo cotton veil/turban covering his head and face from mid-nose downward. He pivoted before the couple considered eye-contact permission to approach, only to bump into a leggy Irma La Douce who promptly fluttered her lashes in a way he was only too used to. Before flirtation spilled from her eyes to her lips, he murmured a few gentle words to make it clear he'd appreciate being left alone.

As the prostitute with the heart of gold moseyed on, tossing disappointed looks back at him, he sighed. He hoped to avoid all attention from now on. Although he'd sponsored this affair, he hadn't invited any of the acquaintances he liked and respected. Instead he had filled the room with people he either barely knew or didn't care much for, to create an anonymous, easily ignored crowd. He was here to focus on and garner the attention of only one person. Farah Beaumont.

Now if only the damned woman would make an appearance.

Suddenly, something sizzled at the back of his neck.

Tensing, he homed in on the source of the disturbance. It was emanating from the giant ballroom doors ten feet away. He turned, imbuing his movement with unconcern.

In the next second, everything lost momentum. His body. His

heart. The world itself decelerated before it vanished. Nothing remained but the creature framed in the intricately gilded doorway, swathed in an ethereal gown made of every shade of green right out of his kingdom's fairy tales. The subject of a fantasy painting come to life.

This was...*her?*

He blinked, as if coming out of hypnosis.

What was he *thinking?* Of *course* it was her. He'd had enough close-ups of her pinned on his wall as he'd prepared for this campaign. Pictures that included several of her wrapped around her sugar daddy, flaunting the nature of their relationship. He knew how she looked, down to the last detail.

Or so he'd thought. Her flesh-and-blood reality far transcended the composite image her photos had created.

None had come close to translating the hundred shades that spun the bronze silk of her hair. None had been faithful to the richness of the thick cream that was her skin. None had hinted at the hue and depth of her eyes. In the most revealing close-ups they'd been a mundane green. But even at this distance, they rivaled the summer meadows and emerald shores of his island put together. And her tailored features echoed no one's, her air implied an individuality so unique that must be encoded in her very genes.

Her photos had misconstrued a combination that he could only describe as...*breathtaking.*

He blinked again. *What are you* thinking, *you fool? She is a self-serving, gold-digging creature inhabiting a siren's body. A body she sells to the highest, most undemanding bidder.*

He gave himself a further mental shake as he watched her proceed across the ballroom, turning every head but noticing no one herself.

Yes, *there* it was, the famed frost.

Yet...maybe not.

It wasn't haughtiness he detected, the despising of all else who lived. It was something he recognized only too well. The bone-deep wish for solitude, the elemental drive to avoid crowds, loathing to be the center of attention yet knowing he was forever doomed to be in it....

There he went again! Assigning not only human traits to the woman who thought nothing of standing aside as a prosperous kingdom descended into chaos, but deeply personal ones, too.

Enough. Time to put things in motion. This was going to be hard and ugly and, if he found no way out, permanent. No reason to draw out the preliminary discomfort.

He signaled to his waiters.

He moved to intercept her, his steps long and leisurely, their steady momentum detailing his intention to bypass her on the way to the French windows leading out onto the terrace.

Five paces from their intersection point, he cast his gaze in a sweeping motion, not intending it to pause on her. The next moment his intentions scattered, along with his ordered thoughts, as his gaze locked on to hers with all the greed and willfulness of everything male in him.

E'lal jaheem. To hell with this. What was he doing deviating from the set plan?

His eyes clung to hers, disregarding his fury at the unprecedented loss of control. Then, at the height of his frustration, he saw it. Reflected in the depths of her gemlike eyes.

Awareness. Startled, rivaling his own, surpassing it for being taken unawares.

The coolness of satisfaction spread behind his sternum.

So—the Ice Queen wasn't immune to him, eh?

With her reputation, he'd been worried she'd be the exception, forcing him to exert himself to catch and keep her attention. It seemed she just hadn't met a man who warranted it.

But she'd met him now.

So maybe she'd relent if she found out *he* was her intended groom, that she'd exchange one billionaire tycoon for another who could more than give her what she needed in bed, things her aging lover surely wasn't providing her with…

What was he thinking? No matter how magnificent she was as a female, she was immoral, heartless. He would never keep her in his bed longer than it took for her to conceive the vital heir.

Based on all he knew of her, he assumed that one factor in her adamant refusal to change her current situation was that she had no desire to lose the freedom of being in control of an older man without giving anything back, giving nothing up. Entering a marriage of state, where she'd be forever monitored and unable to mess around as she no doubt did now, must be unthinkable to her. A man in his prime, who'd keep her toeing the line and in his bed, was certainly to be avoided at all costs.

No. Disclosing his true identity to someone who was as ruthless a businesswoman as he was a businessman would only backfire.

His original plan was the only way to go.

His eyes had remained glued to hers all through his inner deliberations. Voluntarily, he insisted on telling himself, to ascertain her reaction to him.

And he was certain now. He'd never seen such a blatant confession of instant hunger in a woman's eyes. He struggled not to acknowledge the flare of equal hunger in his gut, to keep all turmoil from his eyes. Smugness, hot and triumphant, surged as she faltered to a standstill under the brunt of his approach.

Then his two accomplices collided into them.

Farah Beaumont had been roasting with mortification.

Every eye in the packed, suffocatingly opulent ballroom had

turned at her entrance, the whispers rising over the orchestral music like the hissing of a thousand cobras.

Which wasn't an exaggeration, really. She felt as if she'd just stepped into a pit of snakes. But then, she'd invited their poison when she'd agreed to pose as Bill's lover. Sometimes their purposes in setting up this charade didn't seem worth the malice she met everywhere. Only sometimes, though. She'd found peace since Bill had become her shield and she'd become his payback to his cheating wife. Her predators were now the gossiping, backstabbing kind. The seducing, exploiting kind usually kept their distance, where she wanted them to remain. Where she hoped they'd remain tonight, now that she was here alone.

Damn Bill for insisting she arrive at this *balle-masqué*-cum-fund-raiser farce ahead of him. As if he could resolve the out-of-the-blue catastrophe that had sent their current multi-billion-dollar deal back to square one in time to catch up with her.

But he'd thought it imperative she make an appearance as his representative. God forbid their host—a Middle Eastern magnate who'd sprung out of the shrouds of mystery just a month ago, exploding onto the world-finance scene a fully fledged global player—would feel slighted that a fellow tycoon hadn't graced his self-congratulatory function. Or sent a proxy. It just wasn't done, one world-mover to another. And then, Bill was dying to meet the guy. He was convinced the mystery mogul would make an appearance this time.

She thought he wouldn't. He'd been manipulating the media and the highest circles of finance like a master puppeteer. He was still brewing maneuvers that would change the course of whole regions' economies. She figured he'd reveal himself only when he'd achieved his full plan. Maybe not even then.

Wise man. Got his head screwed on right. Who in their right

mind with that kind of power would squander the blessing of anonymity? What kind of sick psyche wanted the exposure?

She winced. She had to ask that, here, in the presence of
about two thousand such psyches?

It could still have been endurable—come here, meet the guy,
convey Bill's excuses—*if* Bill hadn't insisted she dress up in this
stupid costume.

The image reflected at her after she'd wrestled it on had made
her burst out laughing. For someone who felt clumsy in anything
but casual pants and flats, a Scheherazade costume was a
woefully hilarious misrepresentation. But Bill had really wanted
to make an entrance with her, flaunt her to maximum effect.

Then, as she'd taken the first steps into that sea of malicious
speculation, wishing the floor would snap open and snatch her
into its maw, a pair of lasers had slammed into her.

OK. Exaggeration alert. The so-called lasers were just eyes.
A man's obsidian eyes.

But, no. Lasers weren't an exaggeration. Rather an understate-
ment. She *did* feel as if they were burning her from the eyes
inward… *Whoa. Look away, moron.*

She couldn't. Couldn't break away from the thrall of those
eyes to look at their owner. All she registered beyond the black-
on-white gaze were impressions of toughness, power, size…and
sheer unadulterated maleness.

Her body heat rose, fueled by the frantic engine that had
replaced her heart behind her ribs.

For God's sake! She didn't *do* burning up and instant paraly-
sis. And never, *ever,* instant X-rated thoughts.

Tell that to her malfunctioning volition and heat-regulating
centers. Not to mention her short-circuiting imagination. *That*
became crowded with images of hard virility pressing down on
her, of hot breath singeing her lips, her neck, lower…

Her muscles twitched, sweat broke out on her palms and feet, trickling between her breasts…

Suddenly something slammed into her right shoulder. Then far more than a trickle of liquid was gushing, everywhere.

Chilled shock doused her, freeing her from the man's eyes. Her own flew wide to watch the chain-reaction she'd triggered.

Her sudden halt right in his path had brought him to an abrupt stop, too. And two waiters with trayfuls of champagne had crashed right into them.

She watched in petrified horror as dozens of flutes spilled all over him, felt the echoing scenario all over her, each hit of cold liquid knocking the breath out of her. Then the flutes succumbed to the pull of gravity and hurtling to the floor.

The music swelled, obscuring the medley of smashing crystal as a lull gripped their immediate crowd, that sick fascination with others' humiliation that never ceased to baffle her. The last flute shattered melodically on the glossy parquet floor among the last chords of the concerto.

In the post-finale hush, there was an outburst of apologies from the waiters, of inquiries from bystanders as a dozen hands dabbed at her clothes.

Disoriented at having so many people encroaching on her, her voice rose. "It's OK…thanks…just…*thank* you."

Her words had no effect as six men, the waiters among them, crowded her, insisting on imposing their help on her. She felt her anti-crowd discomfort rising, taking on a phobic edge. She turned to the one presence that wasn't invading her personal space. The man. This time the burning of his gaze was welcome, a refuge.

Understanding her unspoken appeal, he put himself between her and her harassing helpers, cut them off from her with the impressive barrier of his sand-gold-clad body, an imperial flick of his hand sending them scattering from her field of vision. Then he turned to her.

She averted her eyes this time, feeling the heat that had been doused by shock and champagne surging up to her face again.

She'd better not be blushing. She *couldn't* be blushing. She hadn't blushed since she was sixteen.

But the sizzling was unmistakable. She *was* blushing.

Just great. This man was resurrecting every clumsy foolishness she'd thought buried along with her father…who'd turned out to be *not* her real father. Not that biology mattered to her. Francois Beaumont would always remain her father in every way that mattered. And his death over a decade ago had forced her to mature overnight….

Oh, whom was she kidding? She'd matured in certain areas only, had become an expert in erecting barriers and bulldozing her way through the confrontations that made up social life, using her blunted social skills as a weapon.

Now no barrier or battering ram would do, and here she was, soaked, blushing and feeling terminally silly.

As if in answer to her distress again, the man handed her napkins, shielded her from prying eyes as she dried herself, echoing her actions, his movements slower, more efficient.

When he judged she'd done all she could, he retrieved the napkins from her numb fingers, piled them on the trays of the still-apologizing waiters. Then he motioned to her, a graceful gesture that was a cross between command and courtesy, spreading his *abaya's* sleeve like the wing of a great vulture, signaling for her to precede him in the direction he'd been heading when she'd caused the indoor champagne shower.

She didn't need a second bidding, streaked to the open French windows.

As they stepped out into the night, the first solo violin strings of a poignant composition she didn't recognize flowed, as if scoring their progress across the gigantic terrace. Lost in the surreal movielike moment, she breathed in relief. She'd made it outside without snagging those damned spiked heels into that double-damned layered skirt and falling flat on her face.

She felt him two steps behind her, his aura magnified now that others weren't diluting it, felt dwarfed, inundated. She looked around, anywhere but at him, not really seeing the landscaped grounds that sprawled into the moonlit horizon.

Feeling like a ten-year-old who'd just made an irrevocable fool of herself in front of the one person she wanted to make an impression on, she tucked champagne-drenched tendrils behind her ear and blurted out, "Well, that was sure needed."

A smile soaked his fathomless tones as they rode the sultry California summer breeze, a bit muffled behind his intimidating, incredibly exciting veil. "The fresh evening air? The escape from oversolicitous admirers and pawing champagne blotters?"

British. His accent. Highly educated, deeply cultured, laden with class and control. And with an inflection that told her he wasn't actually English, but something too complex to fathom. He sounded exactly as he looked. Exotic, superior, formidable.

Not that she knew how he looked. After the stolen glimpse at his costume—that of someone ready to tackle a sandstorm head-on—she hadn't ventured another look at him. Couldn't work up the nerve to take that look. Probably would only when he decided she'd taken enough of his party time and went back to his companion.

He just *had* to have a companion. Men like him—assuming other men like him existed—were invariably spoken for. And this one wouldn't merely be spoken for. He'd be fought over, tooth and nail.

She sighed. "Actually, I meant the champagne shower."

Hell. And he'd know she wasn't even joking. She should just

shut up until he moved on. She'd do well to remember she was an outcast for a reason. She'd never developed the art of conversation. Or the common sense of social graces. Every time she hurled out what she was thinking, uncensored, she varied between cultivating disgruntled critics or outright enemies.

Not that she was cultivating either here. The man must simply think her a total moron by now. Oh, well.

Turning her back on him, she flopped her purse over her back, raised her multilayered skirt, wrung its ends, took off one soggy shoe, then the other and dangled each over the marble balustrade, watering the shrubs with excess champagne before placing the shoes facedown to drain.

So what if she was confirming his suspicion that he'd just stumbled on the party clown? What did his opinion matter, anyway?

Suddenly, *nothing* seemed to matter as dark rumbles rose, harmonizing with a cello solo, both male and instrumental music enveloping her in a surge of warmth and...well being?

Oh, wow. He was laughing. And not at her. *With* her. She could tell by the answering exuberance rising inside her.

She felt him leaning against the balustrade, looking down at her, and she shivered at the amusement still staining his voice. "So—you welcomed the cooling off, even at the price of braving the rest of the ball wet and sticky, in a ruined gown and barefoot?"

Her lips twisted in self-deprecation. "With the way I was sweating, this was my fate anyway. I was already squishing in my shoes. It was a relief to fast-forward to the inevitable end."

"May I inquire why such a cool-looking butterfly was sweating buckets in the perfectly air-conditioned ballroom?"

Butterfly? At five-foot-six and a hundred and forty pounds, she was too substantial to be called that. And cool-looking? Was he baiting her? Trying to get her to admit why she'd been so hot and bothered? As if she'd tell him!

Then she opened her mouth. "Are you a different species? Perfectly air-conditioned? Not according to this body's thermostat. I entered that ballroom and almost got knocked off my feet by thousands of people emitting the steam of body heat and self-importance, then you trained those eyes on me and I just about spontaneously combusted…"

Shut up. Just shut up.

This was far worse than her usual candor crises. This man disturbed her. Unbalanced her. Big time. But there was no use feeling bad about it now. The damage had already been done.

She gritted her teeth and waited for his response, expecting him to burst out laughing for real this time. Or to take advantage of her confession and proposition her.

"So *that* was why you welcomed the cold shower!" Here it came. The making fun of her. The lewd proposition. Or both. "Thank you."

Wha…? Thank you? What the hell was he thanking her for? The ego stroke? The comic relief?

Her chagrin evaporated as he went on, something that was no longer amusement—wonder?—coloring his magnificent voice. "Thank you for giving me the opening to let you know how *you* tampered with *my* temperature the moment you trained *these* eyes on me."

He touched her then, a thumb tracing a burning, downcast lid then a forefinger below her chin, coaxing her face up. She trembled at the barely substantial contact.

Then he exhaled a gravelly, "Do it again."

His invocation raised her eyes to his without volition. And the impact was even harder this time. In the full moon's rays, the whites of his eyes shone silver, the irises infinite by contrast, a black hole sucking her whole into it.

Then he began unraveling the intricately folded cloth that

obscured his face in slow, hypnotic movements. At last he stopped, dropped his arms to his sides and whispered, sounding as disturbed as she felt, "Look at me. All of me."

His command/plea shattered the spell that had been keeping her eyes captive to his, and she obeyed, letting her gaze stumble all over him, absorbing everything about him with the same greed her gown had soaked up the champagne.

And he was magnificent.

But…no. He was more than that.

Long ago, when she'd believed she'd one day find love and passion with one person who'd been made for her and she for him, she'd had a vague, impossible vision of that person. This man surpassed even that spawn of an outlandish teenage imagination.

Tall, dark and handsome were givens. The devil was definitely in the details here. *How* tall, for instance—ten or more inches taller than her. And though his getup only hinted at his body's power, she'd bet he'd fill out a superhero's suit to perfection. Then came the part of just *how* handsome he was.

She'd never had a knack for poetry or art. She was all about numbers and spreadsheets and harsh financial facts. But she could see how a face like that deserved sonnets. And a wingful of portraits in a museum. His perfect face proved that asymmetrical, weathered faces didn't have a monopoly on character.

But what was really unfair was that his attraction went far beyond the physical. The way his gorgeous eyes spoke, communicated, the command he had over his every move and intonation, the influence he'd displayed on others, herself foremost among them. This was a man who had mental faculties as razor-sharp as his cheekbones.

OK. Something was officially wrong with her.

Was it possible she'd absorbed the dozen glasses of champagne subdermally? She'd gotten drunk once. She'd had an unstoppable urge to blurt out the truth unprovoked then, too.

She succumbed to the urge now. "God, you're beautiful!"

She winced, bit her lip. But it was out. All she could do now was wait for him to shake his head and turn away, to burst into belated laughter or to finally pick up the invitation he must by now believe she was blatantly issuing.

When none of her predictions came true as his scrutiny stretched, she finally snapped, "Take your cue from me, will you? Just spit out whatever you're thinking, then be on your way."

Shehab stared at her. This was completely unexpected.

She was…an absolute surprise. A shock.

The woman the reports and pictures had painted in such clear and cruel detail was nowhere to be found. This woman decimated their assertions and his preconceptions with every move she made, every word she uttered. Her very vibe transmitted a totally alien entity to the one he'd thought he'd have to contend with.

Or she could be the world's best actress.

Not that it mattered what she was.

Whether she was demon or angel or anything in between, his mission remained unchanged.

But something else *had* changed.

Until he'd laid eyes on her, he'd been sick with projecting the various forms of revulsion he'd have to endure on this quest. He'd consoled himself that the throne of Judar was worth his very life and more, not only his freedom.

But now what he'd thought would be an abhorrent duty was looking more and more as though it was going to be a decadent indulgence. Now he couldn't wait to give his all to her seduction.

And entrapment.

Two

She was getting away.

He'd gaped at her too long and she'd gotten fed up. Or angry. With what sounded like a curse, she reached for her shoes, gathered up her skirt and hopped on one foot to put one shoe on. The moment she had the other on, he knew she'd run away.

He moved into her path, his hands taking hers at the wrists in a clasp that was more pantomime than actual grasp.

He extracted the shoe from her unresisting fingers and her supple arm fell to her side. Then, holding her gaze, he went down in front of her, slow, measured, his hand guiding the hand bunching her skirt in the opposite direction to his descent, in a movement just as leisurely, scraping her leg with the rich layers of tulle and chiffon up to her mid-thigh.

Her knees gave a momentary buckle. With another almost-touch, he eased her back against the balustrade. Only then did he break their eye-lock, let his gaze drift down. His fingers followed, hovering an agonizingly unhurried path over the firm cream of her thigh and leg. Once he reached her bare foot, his fingers paused for a long moment. Then they closed on it.

She gasped a hot, sharp sound, jerked, her toes curling.

Someone in the background gave a lewd hoot. He barely registered it. All he could focus on was her labored breathing, his, drowning out the din drifting from the ballroom. He bit his lip to stem the rising stimulation, savoring the first real touch, marveling at the delicacy in her foot's every line, the strength in every bone. She really was exquisite down to her toes.

He traced each one down to her neat, unpainted toenails, then gave her leg a coaxing push, bent her knee, brought her foot up until its arch rested on his shoulder. She was shaking now, each tremor flowing to his frame through the contact.

From this position, kneeling in front of her, feeling her flailing in his power, he decided it was time to answer her.

"You want to know what I was thinking?" He marveled at the ragged edge lacing his words. A convincing simulation of stirred sincerity. He wasn't sure what it was. Excitement? Exhilaration? Arousal? Probably all three. "I was thinking it was you who the word *beautiful* has been coined for. I was thinking that *you* must be a different species, that you put me to shame."

"I do?" she croaked. Then she jerked. "Listen, I—I said some embarrassing stuff…more so than the gems that usually dribble from my big mouth. So…sorry, OK? Just forget them and…" The rest was muffled as she tried to extract her foot from his grip.

He only slid her foot down to his heart level, pressed it there, so lightly he let her know she could escape if she wanted, let her know she couldn't. "Don't apologize. Never apologize. You misunderstand me. You put me to shame with your candor. And then, how could I forget what you said? When I never want to?

I never met a woman, or anyone for that matter, who was anywhere near this delightfully plainspoken."

"Delightfully? Don't you mean painfully? At least, it's painful for me…or more so for me, this time…"

He'd never seen emotions so visibly invading a skin so perfect before. His gaze clung to the progression of her blush, watched the stain of stimulation spreading, taking on a mystical tint in the moonlight. His own blood rushed to his head, to his loins. He raised her clammy foot, dueled with the urge to kiss it, to suckle her toes. An urge he'd never imagined before. He clamped down on it, settled for fitting her shoe back on, a tremor invading his fingers as he slipped her supple foot into the emerald satin-covered creation. It had to be the control he was exerting, so he wouldn't obey his instincts' insistence that he heave up and crush this exquisite female in his arms.

He settled for a whispered lip brush on the inside of her calf, then, with a pang of regret, he let her skirt fall over her creamy flesh, and placed her foot down on the ground. "Why should it pain you, my Cinderella? Doing me such a favor?"

She teetered, grasped her support harder. "Favor?"

He rose slowly, drawing out the moment, the movement, both more potent for his letting her sense his leashed desire without touching her. "A huge one. The moment I laid eyes on you, I wondered how I'd approach you without seeming predatory. Afterward, I wondered if it was wise to tell you how I welcomed the dousing and the chance it gave me to be with you. I went through a list of roundabout ways to tell you what you make me feel without offending you or scaring you off. And here you are, showing me that no maneuvers are needed. Not when what we feel is mutual."

She shook her head as if to clear it. "It is? But—but I don't even know how *I* feel."

He touched a heavy lock of wet bronze silk, oh so close to her breast. "Why don't you describe it to me?"

She pressed against the balustrade, to escape his influence, her desire to press into *him* instead. He knew it. "I—I already told you…you make me feel confused and clumsy…"

"And hot," he finished, elation rising higher.

"Yeah, that, too…" She stopped, groaned. "I don't know why I'm telling you this…apart from the fact that I have this mind-to-mouth incontinence disease…when it's not business stuff…" She paused, seemed to struggle for breath, then burst out again. "This is ridiculous. This has to be the full moon…or the champagne. I'm not *this* socially handicapped."

He leaned closer, pressing his advantage. "This is not social. This is you and me. The moon has nothing to do with the magic brewing between us. It's only shedding a stronger light on it. The champagne, we only bathed in."

"Yeah. Maybe it's champagne-fumes intoxication?"

He had to chuckle. He wanted to remain intense and focused, but everything she said stimulated his humor as much as his libido. "Intoxication is right. You're just looking for a far-fetched reason when you're right here, a vision from a fairy tale who keeps blurting out the most amazing things."

"A vision? Sure. The word you're looking for is a *sight.*"

And the amazing thing was, he felt she wasn't fishing, that her comment carried conviction. And consternation.

He insisted, his voice lowering, roughening, praise coming easy, flowing true. "A vision. So much more potent for being real. And you think the same about me."

She nodded, without hesitation. Then her eyes squeezed and she groaned again. Was it possible this persona, the one who seemed devoid of even an ounce of feminine wiles, was real?

She echoed his skepticism. "But how can any of this be real? What *is* this, anyway?"

"You know what this is. Something you thought you'd never experience. Something I certainly didn't believe even existed. Instant attraction. Total and brutal."

Her eyes filled with concession, with bewilderment, as the music built to climactic heights, as if underscoring his assertion, a manifestation of the charge building between them.

Suddenly her wavering gaze wrenched from his.

He dragged it back with a touch brooking no resistance. She wasn't dismissing him like she had the fates of two kingdoms.

He closed the remaining inches between them until he was a breath away from imprinting himself all over her. The music rose to a crescendo, then held its breath. He pressed his point home. "Don't try to escape the truth. Acknowledge it."

"How can I? W-we don't even know each other's names."

The music came to a dramatic end, as if punctuating her gasped protest. So…she'd introduced the subject of exchanging personal details. Good. It was time he introduced her to the alter ego he'd created in the past month for this purpose.

"That's easily fixed." He reached for her right hand, so soft and pliant and sweaty, took it to his lips. "My name is Shehab Aal Ajman." He pressed a hot kiss in the middle of her palm. "Now all you have to do to meet your condition for sanctioning our attraction is to tell me yours, *ya jameelati*."

Her eyes widened as she snatched her hand away, fisted it as if it itched, burned. "Is that Arabic?"

"It is…my beauty."

"Oh—oh…*oh*." Her faltering eyes widened. "You're *him? Sheikh* Shehab Aal Ajman? But you can't be!"

"I assure you, I can." His lips spread in satisfaction. "So you know of me. How's that for proof that this is fate at work?"

* * *

Realizations piled up in Farah's mind. But stunned or not, his last statement incited her enough to contradict it.

"Oh, no. Fate's got nothing to do with it. How could I *not* know of the venture capitalist who's been rocking the financial world? In my line of work I know of anyone who's making or has the potential of making waves. And you've been making tsunamis." She exhaled her still-climbing incredulity. "Excuse me as I struggle with my misconceptions. I had this image in my head, and it seems hilarious now side-by-side with the truth…your truth."

"And what was that image that my name and reputation summoned to your imagination?"

"A repulsive blob in traditional Bedouin garb, with a high nasal voice and a painful accent, reeking of musk and…"

Somebody gag and sedate her already.

God. What she'd give to rewind and replay their whole meeting. Not that it would turn out any better. Not without her borrowing someone else's personality along with the gown.

But wonder of wonders, instead of looking affronted, Shehab—whose name now summoned only heated visions of virility and sweeping strength—seemed even more amused. "You mentioned a line of work. You actually *work?*"

She raised one eyebrow, hackles priming to rise. "Yeah, I work. In fact, I don't do much besides work. And the reason behind the condescending disbelief would be?"

"Looking at you in this gown fit for the head concubine in a sultan's harem, my Scheherazade, it's hard to believe you're anything but some blessed man's pampered possession."

Chagrin shot up inside her. Just as she was about to spit out an obliterating comeback, she realized what he was doing.

"Oh…you're…Oh! OK…touché," she mumbled. "I deserved that."

His smile became all indulgence. "Yes, you did." He wound a lock of her hair around his forefinger. "So what is this work that's taken over such a vibrant siren's life?"

She pretended to look around, her heart skipping. "Siren? Where? Me? Man, this gown is really projecting a false image." She huffed in irony. "Far from being a siren as the costume suggests—and it was imposed on me, by the way—I have what has to be the world's most un-sirenlike job. I'm head financial advisor for Bill Hanson of Global View Finance."

His eyebrows lifted slightly. Was he impressed? Not? What?

His comment didn't even hint at his opinion. "Sounds as if you find the position…lacking. Why do it then?"

She shrugged. "I know nothing else. My father—uh, adoptive father, as I lately discovered—inhabited the world of high finance, and he raised and bred me to live there. After he died, it was even more imperative that I walk in his footsteps. But by the time I was old enough to take over his business, there was nothing left. So I'm lucky to have landed such a position. I never thought about whether it appeals to me or not. I just do the best job I possibly can."

Something fired in his eyes. It was gone in seconds, but it made her rush to add, "Listen…about those things I said a minute ago. That was one piece of prejudiced garbage. So, I'm sorry, not only for harboring it, but for actually voicing it—"

His hand rose in a silencing gesture, before he turned it, swept the back of his fingers sensuously across her lips. "What have I told you about apologizing? Never ever, *ya helweti.*"

She squinted down at the hand feathering her flesh, the perfection of long, strong fingers encased in taut bronze, adorned with just the right amount and pattern of silky black hair. Her mind crowded with images of nuzzling those fingers, suckling them. And as if his touch wasn't enough, there were the foreign words he kept scalding her with, the way the mobile sculpture of his lips embraced them, the way his awesome voice caressed them...

Her blood tumbled in a spin cycle. "Another endearment?"

Great. She sounded like a fish thrashing out of its bowl. Probably looked it, too.

He gave a nod, deceptively lazy, laden with so much heat and temptation. "My sweet. And you are, so unbelievably sweet, every word you say, everything you do. I can't wait to find out if your sweetness runs through and through." He suddenly stood straighter, obliterated the breath between them, let her feel him, if only in whisper touches along all of her. It felt as if his magnetic field was all that kept her upright. "But you haven't told me your name yet. I need to know it. I need to murmur it against your lips, against every inch of you, taste it with your nectar, get high on it as I do on you. Tell me."

She tried to find her voice, her name, but couldn't. She was being swept away, the shores of reason receding. She saw nothing but his eyes, his lips, wanted nothing but for them to fulfill his promise, taste her, possess her, devour her.

But he was waiting, insisting on finding out her name, as per her idiotic objection, before he acted on his promises.

Just tell him. She did, gasped it, "Farah..."

His sharp intake of breath felt as if it tore into her own lungs, flooding her with his scent. "Farah. An Arabic name. This *is* fate. And your parents knew just what you'd be. Joy."

She'd always smirked at the meaning of her name. Apart from the sporadic times of contentment in the company of her ultra-busy father, she'd never experienced anything approaching joy.

She gave a laugh, shaky, self-deprecating. "Not according to my mother. I certainly haven't been her joy."

"Of course you were. How could you not be?"

"And to answer that, I'll have to refer you to her."

His frown was spectacular. "She actually told you that you are not the joy of her life? What mother says that to her child?"

"A mother who turned out to have lived a much more complicated life than I dreamed possible. I guess I was the reminder of my real father. *Not* a source of happy thoughts."

He cupped her cheek. Was his hand on fire? She pressed into his palm, wanting to burn. His hand pressed back before going to her nape, tilting up her head. "She had no right to taint your life, to let her emotions for you be polluted by her bitterness against your biological father."

She pressed her head harder into his assuagement. "Oh, she never said anything like that. It's my own conclusion. You see, she's always been morose, withdrawn. She does everything right, but it's all…held back, as if she's going through a chore, finding no…joy—there's that word again—in it. When I learned about my real father, it made sense. She loved him beyond reason it seems, and was never the same after losing him."

A long moment passed as he stared at her, his face a blank mask. At last he exhaled. "So you don't feel bitter toward her? Or toward your real father for scarring her, making her less than the perfectly loving mother that you deserved?"

"I don't do bitterness. What does it serve?"

"Indeed. So, not only a siren, but a deeply sane one, too."

She coughed a laugh. Sane? Not that *she'd* noticed since she'd laid eyes on him.

"Is your real father alive? Do you now know who he is?"

"Yeah, to both questions. I found out over a month ago. And let me tell you, it's been one hell of a roller-coaster ride."

"Care to elaborate?"

"Uh…I'd appreciate it if we change the subject. It ranks right up there with tearing my skin on barbed wire." And she wasn't exaggerating. If anything, she was understating how discovering her real parentage had left her feeling. Her world had blown apart when her mother had dropped the bomb that Francois Beaumont wasn't her father—that some Middle Eastern monarch was. Then her newfound father, King Atef of Zohayd, had overwhelmed her with his happiness at finding her, his eagerness to know her— his long-lost daughter. And she'd found herself responding, liking him, waiting with baited breath for his next call or message. She'd worried about her eager reaction, wondering if she was desperate for a new father figure to fill the gaping void her adoptive father's death had left inside her. But King Atef had swept her up in his excitement, soothing her worry that she was betraying her dad's memory by being so happy to find another father. Then he'd come to meet her and had dropped another bomb. He needed her to marry some prince from a neighboring kingdom as part of a political pact.

And she'd realized that it had been another setup. Another lie. He was just another man pretending emotions he didn't feel, saying whatever it took to get her to go along with his self-serving plans. She'd shut him and his protestations of sincerity out, kept hoping he'd find another easy way to put his pact through so he'd stop badgering her, so he'd forget she existed....

Shehab trailed a forefinger along her forearm, jogging her out of her oppressive musings before tears of letdown and heartache and guilt spilled from her eyes again.

"It hurt that much?"

"Actually, tearing my skin didn't hurt that much."

His eyes flared. "How? When?"

Her bones rattled with the blast of response to his intensity. "You mean the wound? Uh, I was trying to sneak under a fence on one of my father's ranches and got caught on the barbed wire. I was eleven."

"Where?"

"O-on my back…" She barely held back the rest, the other wound she'd sustained on her left buttock when she'd panicked and struggled to free herself.

"Show me."

It wasn't a request. It was a demand. A demand she didn't even think of denying. She could only close her eyes, turn.

And his hands were on her. Spanning her waist, removing the cascade of her hair, exposing the dipping back of her dress.

His hands skimmed her skin as he searched for the healed evidence of her injury. She stood mute, unable to tell him he wouldn't find it there. He didn't need to be told. He eased her zipper down, the sound, the idea of what he was doing, what she was letting happen, almost making her keel over.

He traced warm, knowing fingers down her spine until they met the slightly raised scar above her tailbone. She keeled over then, over the balustrade, swamped in sensation. He traced its outline, and the tissue that alternated between numbness and aching fired with stimulation. Each caress sent lightning forking throughout her body, lodging in her nipples and core.

"Does it still hurt?" His fingers traveled up and down to the rhythm of his words, yanking the direction of the electric current lancing through her back and forth until she almost collapsed. She could only shake her head. Shake, period.

"Tell me you never hurt yourself again." His palm splayed over her scar in a gesture rich with something far more disturbing than lust. Concern, protection. What she'd never felt from anyone but her father and Bill. And to feel it from him…

She shook her head again, heard a satisfied rumble deep in his chest before he ended his torture, pulled the zipper up. Then he clamped her waist again, turned her to him, bore down on her with his aura and hunger.

And she couldn't move. Couldn't breathe. Had to be totally still, to watch him do it, take the first taste of her.

But he didn't do it. His lips descended only to whisper against her burning cheek, "*Ya ajmal makhloogah ra'ayta'ha,* the most beautiful creature I've ever seen, dance with me."

Dance? *Dance?* That was all he wanted?

But she wanted more. He'd been right. She'd never imagined she could feel anything like this. Hunger that rocked her, frightened her, made her crave things from him she'd never wanted from another man. Things she'd *hated* from other men.

But he was only drawing her into a loose embrace, leading her into the first languid steps of a waltz. Maddening her with enough contact to inflame her more, but not enough to blunt the talons of need that sank deeper into her flesh with every move.

To her surprise, she felt her feet flowing into steps learned during her days as her father's favorite dance partner. Then the rest of her body followed, as one with the rhythm, with his every move, with him. She felt grace and power pulsing in her arms as she wound them around his steel bulk, securing him to her. She had a feeling it would all end when the dance was over. She was taking all she could…now.

At one point, Shehab groaned against her temple, "You *are* the meaning of your name. This would be how a *hooreyah,* one of the inhabitants of heaven who brings total joy, would feel in my arms…" He pressed her harder to his length. "But, no. If those creatures do exist, they'd be nothing to you. With you, it's like dancing with bliss, with passion made human."

Laughter flowed from her, unfettered, delirious. She didn't believe any of those things applied to her, but it seemed he believed they did. Why not, when she believed the same about him? This had to be what he'd said it was. Magic. And she wouldn't think how or why. She'd just wallow in it.

Somewhere in her hazy mind she realized the music had ended, another piece had started and they were no longer dancing. He was leading her down the wide marble steps to the gardens. And she was following him, still laughing, ready for anything. She felt like someone coming out of stasis and now rushing toward the first moments of life.

He took her behind obscuring trees, pressed her against a smooth trunk, then took her face in both hands. In a rogue moonbeam slashing among the foliage, his face and obsidian gaze were supernatural in beauty, in impact. She felt penetrated, the notion of spontaneous combustion no longer such an impossibility anymore.

Just as she thought she'd crumble to his feet in ashes she cried out, *"Shehab…"*

He swallowed his name, growled hers inside her. "Farah…"

And it was like opening a floodgate. She'd thought nothing could be better than his feel and scent. His taste was. She wanted to drown in it. She *was* drowning. In kisses that gave her glimpses of the ferocity she needed from him. His hands joined in her torment, gliding all over her, never pausing long enough to appease, until she writhed against him, whimpering, begging, not really knowing what she was begging for, "Shehab…*please…*"

His lips clamped down on hers then, moist, branding, his tongue thrusting deep, singeing her with pleasure, breaching her with need, draining her of moans and reason.

She took it all, not knowing what to do to pleasure him in turn. It was just so…so…*everything.* Pressure built, in her eyes, chest, loins. Her hands convulsed on his arms until he relented, lowered her zipper, pushed her gown and purse strap from her shoulders, setting her swollen breasts free.

She keened. With relief, with the spike in arousal. He had her exposed, vulnerable. Maddened. *"Please…"*

Her hands pressed her breasts together to mitigate their aching as everything inside her surged, gushed, needing anything...*anything* he would do to her. His fingers and tongue and teeth exploiting her every secret, his body all over hers, his manhood filling the void between her thighs, thrusting her to oblivion...

Oh, God. What was she thinking?

She wanted him to do all that to her? There? Then?

What was wrong with her?

Then revelation came. *Nothing* was wrong with her.

Something...*everything*...was finally right.

This was all wrong.

He was supposed to be the one performing the seduction.

He was always the one in control, easily taking what was on offer or leaving it, his libido never in the driver's seat.

No woman had ever had him a breath away from insanity.

But as his eyes glazed over kiss-swollen lips and glistening eyes, over the perfection of full breasts pressed together in a mind-blowing offering, he couldn't remember how this had started, or why he shouldn't take what his body was bellowing for, come what may.

He'd been wrong about her. This unpredictable enchantress was nothing like the hardened vixen he'd expected.

And she was infinitely more dangerous for it.

And it didn't matter to him. Nothing did. Not her crimes or that she was another man's mistress, who, an hour after meeting *him,* was begging him to do anything and everything to her. It only inflamed him more, the force of her equal hunger...

No. *No.* He couldn't give her what she wanted that easily.

If he did, he'd be a one-night stand to her. A steady supply of those *had* to be how she filled her insatiable sexual needs.

Although she'd been discreet, no doubt fearing her lover's wrath. His reports on her hadn't included any known liaisons.

But she was pressing into him, all that glorious passion and flesh. He could smell her arousal, feel it vibrating in his loins, hear it thundering in his cells. Surely this much hunger wouldn't be satisfied with one frenzied mating. He could take her now and it would only start her addiction, as he'd planned…

No. He couldn't risk it. He had to stop. Even if he wasn't sure his potency would survive the blow.

"Farah, wait." She didn't heed him, her lips at his pulse wringing coherence from his body. He tried again, his voice a gruff groan he didn't recognize. "We have to stop…"

And again her reaction was nothing he could have predicted. It was as if he'd shot her. She jackknifed away, stumbling as she fumbled to pull up her gown and purse, emotions slashing across her face. Shock, frustration, embarrassment. It was the distress that disturbed him. A distress she must surely be feigning.

Before he could say anything she rasped, "You have someone in there…or somewhere, don't you? I should have asked…" She stopped, her mortified gaze hardening into a glare. "Wait a minute. I'm less to blame here than you." She struck his hands off. "What kind of a bastard remembers his commitment to another woman just before…What kind of promiscuous jerk *starts* a—a situation like this when-when…"

Kettle calling the pot black, anyone? But then, now wasn't the time to let her know that he knew she was a two-timer herself.

He clamped her shoulders, wouldn't let her shake him off. "You wait a minute. I have no one waiting for me in there, or anywhere."

Her lower lip trembled. "Really?"

He barely stopped himself from catching that lip, making a feast of it. "Farah, I'm saying this once. I don't have, and have never had, any kind of commitment to any woman."

"Which probably doesn't say much about you."

Her scoffed volley was so unexpected it wrung a surprised laugh from him. "It says I'm free to start a 'situation like this.'" She mumbled something. He frowned. "What did you say?"

She shrugged, her color deepening. "Nothing."

"Farah."

"Listen, I should just shut up, preferably forever, and get the hell out of here. Do me a favor and forget you ever saw me."

"Alf la'nah—a thousand damnations—tell me what you said."

She grumbled some more. Then she sighed. "I said 'Of course you're free to start a situation like this. And to end it. And to hell with your partner, anyway.' Satisfied now?"

He laughed again. *"Enti majnoonah, weh ajeebah*...crazy and incredible." He crowded her against the tree, snatched up her skirt, nudged her thighs apart as he lifted her, brought her down over an erection huge and hard enough for her to straddle. "Does it feel like I want to end this? Anywhere but inside you?"

She gasped as his hardness dug into her core through his *taub* and her sodden panties. Her hands clutched at some branches to hold on to, her legs going around his hips. "Then—then why...?"

He cupped her buttocks, rasped, "Why did I stop? Why aren't we already in the throes of the first orgasm of many?"

His words jolted through her, sent her back arching and her hips grinding down on his erection. Moonlight exploded into fireworks. He would climax, would make her climax if he'd only thrust at her, like this, through their clothes... *No. Stop.*

He disentangled her legs from around his hips, gritted his teeth against the combined force of their frustration, took himself out of range of her scent and hunger.

He stared out into the gardens, still blind. "I can't believe I'm saying this, but this is too fast." He inhaled, struggled to come down. "It's magical and unprecedented, it defies time and timing, but that's why I can't risk spoiling it. I can't rush you into intimacy, no matter how willing you think you are, and cast recriminations or shame or regret on it all."

He paused, dazed at his fluency. He should only be glad the pretense was coming so unaffectedly to him.

He turned to her, pain leveling, his sight back, found her looking smaller, her face shimmering with uncertainty. Stiff steps took him back to her. "I beg of you, *ya ameerati,* let's start again, slowly…slower. Let me see you again…and again."

"Oh, yes, yes, *yes.*"

He couldn't help but laugh. She'd actually whooped, jumped up and down. This couldn't be an act, could it?

But why should he care? It was going his way so easily.

Though maybe he should feel bad, if she wasn't the unfeeling creature he'd been intending to manipulate?

No. He shouldn't. Even if she wasn't acting, only her choices mattered. She'd talked of discovering her real father only in terms of how it had hurt her. She cared nothing for the pain she was causing that father or the damage she was causing his kingdom. She thought of nothing but her own comfort and convenience and, right now, her own pleasure.

Well, he'd make her wait for it. He'd drive her insane wanting it. And when the time was right, he'd take her, ensnare her. Then he'd marry her. Once the marriage was a reality, it wouldn't matter what she thought. Or wanted.

She didn't matter. Only Judar did. Only the throne.

Reiterating the resolve, he rasped, "Let me take you home."

"That would be wonderful…" Her words trailed off and her passion-drugged face fell. "I forgot. I drove here."

"I'll have one of my chauffeurs collect your car." He tugged her to his side, felt a rush as she nestled into him as if she were a missing part. *Focus, ya rejjal. This rubbish is what you say to her, not what you think.* He inhaled. "But don't think I'll leave you on your doorstep. I'll change you out of this ruined gown, wait for you to shower, tuck you in bed, give you a massage, kiss you good-night…"

She trembled, clung tighter, making him wonder if she was far gone enough to say yes to marriage right now.

No. A no from her would be final, and he had no other leverage but her need. And it had to be great indeed for her to consent to marriage according to his culture. One she couldn't terminate in any court of law when she wanted out.

He'd show his hand after he'd entangled her. In every way.

When they reached the parking lot, he reluctantly withdrew the hand he'd found inside her bodice hungrily cupping her breast, pushed a button on a wireless device in his pocket. He took another taste of her lips as he reiterated inwardly, *any moment now.*

Just as Farah was almost climbing him again, the night around them splintered into the bursts of a dozen flashes.

Three

One second, Farah was swathed in Shehab's power and eagerness, buoyed by the promise of the night ahead and so many days and nights to follow. The next she crashed back to reality, as figures materialized out of the void that had existed beyond her and Shehab, shattering their cocoon of intimacy.

It still took the flashes burning her retinas with splotches of painful blindness to make her realize what the figures were. *Paparazzi.*

Helplessness and outrage lurched through her, against the merciless greed of the predators who'd invaded her life countless times, polluted her image and shattered her peace. No matter that she'd practically given them license to do so, with her arrangement with Bill. It still made her ill every time.

They were now catching her in her one moment of unguarded abandon to joy, turning her discovery of Shehab and her own unknown depths into photographic evidence that would turn all the magic into something cheap and sordid.

But before distress bubbled to her lips, Shehab offered her the refuge she hadn't cried for yet, whirling her around, his clothes swirling around him like a magician's cape, enfolding her into what felt like another dimension, where nothing existed but the duet of their heartbeats, hers a cacophony of irregularity, his the very rhythm of steadiness.

Then other sounds invaded her awareness. Stampeding feet, imploding flashes and shouted outrage. She clung to him, her heart invading her throat, breached, under attack.

Then she was no longer touching ground, swept up in his power, the world tilting then bounding on fast, steady thuds.

Suddenly a car screeched to a stop a few feet away from them. A gleaming black stretch limo.

Half a dozen men materialized out of nowhere, one opening the back door for them, the rest surging toward her and Shehab, overtaking them, putting themselves between them and the commotion at their back. Shehab lowered himself inside the spacious vehicle with her still held securely in his arms. The door immediately slammed shut with a muted *oomph* and the limo shot forward soundlessly.

Shehab's hands ran all over her, soothing, caressing her own hands, which ached from clutching him to her.

"It's over," he murmured. "My men will detain them."

She unclenched her grasp on him, squeezed her eyes shut. Yeah, sure. Good luck with that. The paparazzi had already gotten what they'd hounded her for more than two years to obtain—evidence that she was a promiscuous tart who constantly cheated on her sugar daddy. And she'd obliged them this time, leaving a party disheveled and climbing all over a man like a cat in heat.

But it was worse than that. What hurt most was his men. With the way they'd appeared on the spot, they must have been invisibly following Shehab all along, must have seen…everything…

Mortification made her struggle out of his arms, spilled her on the plush leather couch beside him.

She felt sick at heart, at the whole thing, was afraid she'd be sick for real. Her head flopped on the headrest as everything tumbled through her mind in a vicious spin cycle.

"Can you please ask your chauffeur to pull over?"

He hit a button, rapped the order in Arabic. Another button flipped open a compartment from which he produced wet towels, then with utmost gentleness he wiped her face, neck, arms and the tops of her breasts with their fragrant coolness.

Long moments later, he stopped, looked at her. "Better?"

Oh, she was so *not* better. His caresses had at first soothed her, but then they'd become fire, licking exposed nerve endings. Her womb was contracting so hard, it was almost painful.

How could he do this to her? Even now, when she was dying of embarrassment?

She nodded, mutely. Otherwise she'd tell him the exact truth. She'd told him enough of that for one night.

Giving her such a smile, that of an artist looking in satisfaction on his handiwork, he tried to move her again onto his lap. She resisted, and he only coaxed her with more insistent caresses, his lips rubbing against her temple. "Let me soothe you, *ya ja-meelati*. You really are shaken up by the paparazzi's appearance, aren't you?"

"I've developed a phobia where they're concerned," she admitted.

He pressed her harder into his containment. "They've pursued you before?"

* * *

Shehab pulled back when Farah made no response, watched agitation shudder over her face. It felt so real he almost felt sorry for arranging the incident.

The plan had come to him when he'd been informed paparazzi had followed her when she'd left to come to the ball without Hanson, as he'd planned. He'd known they'd swarm the park until she made an exit, hoping to succeed where they'd failed so far, to catch her in one of the infidelities everyone insisted she regularly indulged in. He hadn't been about to risk her slipping and providing them with their coveted photographic evidence, not when he'd have to make her his princess. But he'd decided to use their presence to his advantage.

He'd ordered his men to get rid of the paparazzi, to take their place, to pretend to ambush them on his signal. He'd planned to get her into a compromising position somehow, aiming to convince her that her spotless record of never having been caught in the act was at an end. But even his best projections hadn't included his leaving the ball with her all over him.

He'd almost forgotten to give the signal, had done it with utmost reluctance, hating to have his men witness any measure of their intimacies, even the mild kiss he'd allowed them to see.

He'd expected her to cry out for him to send his men after the paparazzi, to make sure no evidence of her indiscretion remained in existence. He'd gambled on that driving her deeper into his trap, adding the feeling of being partners in barely averted scandal to the mix, compounding desire with debt.

But her response to the whole situation had again thrown him for a loop.

She'd been scared instead of incensed, was now looking so rattled, so pained, he almost blurted out that she had nothing to worry about.

Which proved he was thinking with nothing above the neck.

Yet—why hadn't she made any demands that he contain the situation? Did she assume he would anyway, for *his* reputation?

She at last let out a wavering exhalation. "They've been hounding me since my father—my adoptive father—died." So, no demand yet. When would it come? She went on, her voice strangled with emotion. "They always find a reason for their sick interest in me. I'm just scared witless that this latest episode has something to do with their getting wind that I was adopted, or worse, who my newfound biological father is. If it does, they'll never leave me alone."

He knew he should steer away from this subject, shouldn't risk her connecting him with the situation between her and King Atef. He couldn't resist asking, "Because of the drama of the discoveries? Or is your bioligical father's identity worthy of creating a sensation?"

"Both. Just the fact that Francois Beaumont isn't my father would make them salivate. But oh, boy, is my biological father's identity sensational. If *I* can hardly believe it, imagine what the tabloids would make of it."

He had to be satisfied with that, would recall her answer later for analysis. For now he had to end this strain of thought, divert her to safer grounds.

He shrugged. "They could have been after me."

"But no one knew who you are, except me…"

Her breath left her in a rush. He gritted his teeth at the response its freshness and femininity wrung from him. At the surge of what felt too much like shame.

Anger at the stupid feeling roughened his voice. "Yes."

Her breath caught now. Savoring the depth of the privilege he'd imparted to no one but her? Let her. It was the best way to snare a woman, appealing to her vanity.

Just as he was sure he'd fathomed her reaction, she frowned. "Do you realize how stupid that was? To blow your anonymity like that to someone you just met?"

That was again the last thing he'd expected her to say.

Unsure how to react, he raised an eyebrow. "I trusted you?"

Her glower, her tone, only grew sharper. "And which part of your anatomy made that monumental decision?"

What he'd just been thinking. He shook his head as if it would make this turn in conversation make better sense. "I *have* made it so far by trusting my instincts…"

The irony of his words made him stop. For his instincts were lying. They'd been lying ever since he'd laid eyes on her.

She mistook his pause for belated realization. "See what I mean? So you were right to trust me, but what if you weren't? Worse still, what if someone overheard you on the terrace?"

He stared at her. Anyone would have sworn that she cared. Knew how to care. But he knew better.

"No one heard me. And then no one who does know me could have recognized me. I was covered from the eyes down…"

She huffed a sardonic laugh. "And you consider that a disguise? Do you think anyone wouldn't recognize your eyes? Not to mention your physique. Put them together, and anyone who'd seen you across a street would recognize you."

He was used to women flattering him, knew much of their flattery used truths as ammunition. But he'd always recognized the self-serving intentions behind the adulation. He detected none now in hers, delivered in this no-nonsense, exasperated-at-his-obliviousness way. He barely stopped himself from hauling her on top of him again and showing her how he reciprocated in kind.

Which was probably the effect she'd planned. Or was that as far-fetched as it sounded to him?

Getting more confused, he exhaled. "I was in that ball for over an hour before you arrived. No one recognized me."

"Then the paparazzi were after me." She seemed to deflate beside him. "It's weird, but I'm actually relieved they were." Suddenly she shot up straight again, clutched his forearm. "But— the photos…" Here it came. The belated demand. "They might have taken some of your face. I'm used to being pursued, but I can't bear it if being with me is going to expose you to their viciousness."

And? Where was the demand for him to undo it? For his own privacy and comfort, of course, not hers?

None came. Instead, her eyes suddenly sparkled with moisture and she choked, "I'm so sorry, Shehab."

And he gave in. He lowered his head with a groan, stilled her tremulous words and lips with his, his tongue gliding over her plumpness, unable to wait to plunge into her again. She opened for him with a whimper, overpowering him with her surrender, allowing him all the licenses he needed.

Desire crested, threatening to overcome all considerations. He severed their meld, looked down on her. "Don't be sorry, ever, *ya jameelati*." Then he gave in again, ending his own maneuver, giving her what she hadn't asked for, gaining nothing for himself. "And don't worry, either. Never fear anything when I'm with you. I'd defend you against anything." And he would. Only because she was the key to protecting the throne of Judar, he insisted to himself. "My men will make sure those paparazzi have nothing to publish."

"You mean they'll…? Oh…*oh*." Her eyes widened, the tears stagnating in them, making them gleam like jewels in the semi-darkness. Then tears surged again, dejection replacing agitation in her expression. "Not that that makes me feel any better." It didn't? "The paparazzi probably saw far less than your men did."

It took him a second to understand. She thought his men had witnessed all their intimacies in the gardens.

His outrage felt real even to himself when he growled, "You think I would have almost taken you if my men were all around?"

She blinked, tears receding, if not before two escaped, rolled down the velvet of her cheek. "They weren't?"

"B'Ellahi…" He caught the drops of precious moisture in his mouth, kissed his way to her trembling lips again. "Of course not. I buzzed for them the moment the paparazzi appeared." Which was as near the truth as could be.

This time she sagged in his arms, an exhalation wracking her voluptuous frame. "Thank God. I was mortified thinking they must have seen it all, how it must have looked to them even though it felt like magic to me…"

This was what had so upset her so much? The thought that others had witnessed their lovemaking, defiling the moments of magic with base thoughts and sordid projections?

Not knowing what to think anymore, he pressed her harder to his chest. She surrendered to his caresses for a long moment, then she stiffened by degrees, until she pushed out of his arms, sat up facing him in the prim pose of someone about to deliver an unpleasant message to a total stranger. It was her transparent features that betrayed her real emotions. Embarrassment, awkwardness, hesitation.

"We may have shaken them off, but now that you've deprived them of prime scandal material, they'll be more rabid than ever. They'll be waiting for us back at my place." She suddenly groaned. "Listen, just drop me off at any hotel. I'll spend the night there, then they can photograph me alone to their hearts' content when I return tomorrow after work."

So, the maneuver hadn't led where he'd projected, was now backfiring. He had to improvise a course correction.

He took her hands to his lips slowly, made sure he had her trembling in his power again before he said, "I have a better idea.

The night is still young and we can stall them until they believe you won't go back. Have dinner with me."

Her hand convulsed around the kiss he placed in her palm, her fingers digging in his jaw. He'd kept his eyes on hers all the time, watched as she capitulated under the surge of eagerness for more of him. He still waited until she gasped, nodded her consent. Then he opened the channel to his chauffeur again.

"*Seeda.* To the airport."

"The airport?"

At her croak, Shehab smiled at her, slow and hot. "We're going to have dinner on board my jet."

Of course. Had she thought—if she could still count thinking among her brain functions anymore—that he'd take her to a restaurant, no matter how lavish, or even a yacht or a mansion, as any ordinary tycoon would have done?

He pulled her into a loose embrace and held her all the way to the airport, his hands cascading caresses all over her until she felt he'd scrambled her nervous transmissions forever.

The limo finally stopped and he got out, came around to open her door for her and almost had to carry her limp form out.

She looked dazedly around, realized they were beneath a giant silver-finished jetliner. The warm moisture of the night after the cool dryness of the limo sprouted goose bumps all over her, adding to her imbalance. She was thankful for his support all the way up the Air Force One–style air-stairs that led from the tarmac to the inside of the jet.

She'd been on private jets before. But none had come close to Shehab's. Her father had been a mere multimillionaire who'd had two small jets, and his acquaintances had been on par with him. While Bill, who was as big a multi-billionaire as they came, had started out penniless and to this day couldn't bring himself to spend a penny more than needed to fulfill his needs in terms of function and convenience. It was clear Shehab believed in fulfilling those same needs but spared no expense in pursuit of esthetics and luxury. She said so.

He smiled down at her. "I spend a good deal of my life in the air, and I travel with staff on many occasions. Also, I often don't have the luxury of commuting into the cities I land in and have to conclude all my conferencing and entertaining onboard."

"So you have to have a palace in the sky to do it in, huh?"

He raised one eyebrow. "That's a strange chastisement coming from someone who inhabits the world of high finance."

"Oh, I certainly don't inhabit it. According to whichever of my skills is needed on a given day, I range between being the tarot card reader, the resident nag, the cleaning lady and the…uh…guide dog of the world of high finance."

He tipped his head back and his laughter boomed, sending her heartbeats scattering all over the jet's lush carpeting.

"*Ya Ullah,* will I ever even come close to guessing what you'll say next?" He still chuckled as he led her through many compartments, where his staff hovered in the background, to the spiral staircase leading to the upper deck, all the time casting his enjoyment down on her. "So you consider this jet too pretentious? A waste of money better spent on worthy causes?"

Her lips twisted. "I think any personal item with a telephone number price is ludicrous."

"Not when it's a utility that enables me to steadily make hundreds of millions of dollars more, money I assure you I use in many venues that do serve worthy causes."

Her eyes widened. "I remember now. Many of the global interests you have controlling shares in have varied, not to mention widely effective, aid programs. When I investigated your investment portfolio, I thought to myself, that Aal Ajman guy is trying to build himself a reputation as a philanthropist on par with Bruce Wayne..." She stopped when his laughter boomed again, then mumbled, "It's a relief you're invulnerable to the shrapnel that keeps flying out of my mouth."

"Like Clark Kent, you mean? Very flattering, being likened to two superheroes inside two sentences."

"I did think earlier you'd fill out one of their costumes very nicely..." She groaned, looked up at him helplessly.

His eyes told her how much he enjoyed her uncensored opinions, then his lips brushed her burning cheek. "I am beyond flattered. I want to be a superhero in your eyes, *ya jameelati*."

Only reaching the upper deck stopped her from saying he was. He walked her across an ultrachic foyer and through an automatic door that he opened using a fingerprint recognition module. It whirred shut behind them as he guided her to one of the cream leather couches. She hit the plush surface, looked around the grand lounge drenched in golden lights, earth tones and the serenity of sumptuousness and seclusion. At the far end of the huge space that occupied the full breadth of the jet, a folding screen decorated in Middle Eastern designs of complimenting colors obscured another area behind it.

Shehab bent, brushed her temple with his lips. "This—" he gestured to a door at the other end of the lounge "—is the lavatory. Those buttons access all functions and services. Order refreshments or whatever you wish for until I come back." He straightened up and turned away. Before she could run after him, demanding to be taken wherever he was going, he paused at the lounge's door, added with a deep vocal caress, "I'll rush back to you in minutes."

She slumped back in her seat, closed her eyes for a moment before she took his advice, got up and headed to the lavatory.

She came out to find him waiting for her where he'd left her.

She did a double-take, faltered, gulping air around a lump that materialized in her throat. He'd taken off his costume.

And no. He wasn't naked. But he probably wouldn't affect her more if he was. OK, he would, but it was bad enough now that she wasn't ready to think how much worse it could get. And he was wearing only a simple white shirt and black pants. If anything about him or what he provoked in her could be called simple.

He smiled that slow smile of his, no doubt noting the drool accumulating at her feet. Then he extended a powerful hand in invitation. It felt as if it was by his will alone that she covered the space between them, unable to stop devouring everything about his relatively exposed grandeur, what she'd thought she'd imagined beneath his robes, in unmanageable gulps.

Reality again far outstripped her imagination. The regal shape of his head, the vigorous waves and the deep, dark gloss of his hair accentuated the chiseled sculpture of his face, deepened the hypnosis of his eyes.

She tore hers away from their influence and almost moaned. The breadth of his shoulders and chest had owed nothing to the obscuring clothes and was magnified now that they were covered only in a layer of finest silk. They, and his arms, bulged with power and symmetry under the cloth that hid and detailed at once, both actions wickedly tantalizing. His abdomen was sparse and hard, his waist narrow, as were his hips, before his thighs flowed with strength and virility on the way down to endless legs.

Magnificent was certainly no fitting description. He did far surpass her adolescent visions.

"Come sit down, Farah."

She sat down where the tranquil sweep of his hand indicated. Before she collapsed. The way he said her name, the way he looked at her, the way he moved, breathed, just was—it was all…too much.

He followed her down on the couch, secured her in a seat belt, buckled his own, then turned away as he pressed a button on a remote control-like device. The engines, which she'd just realized had been on for a while now, revved higher and the jet started moving.

But she couldn't even feel surprise.

She felt nothing but her blood freezing inside her veins.

As he'd turned away, she'd caught something in his eyes, something coming over his face.

A maliciousness. A ruthlessness.

Suddenly the ice fractured, and a geyser of alarm scalded through her.

She'd gotten on his plane with him, the plane that was now taking off for only he knew where, someone she'd met just hours ago, trusting him without question, that he was who he'd said he was, that he hid his identity for privacy reasons and not for sinister ones.

But what if she'd been wrong? All along? What if their meeting had more to it that she thought? That he'd targeted her for some reason? Being who she was, at first Francois Beaumont's daughter, then Bill Hanson's right hand, had been reason enough for people, especially men, to target her, each with their own agenda. And Shehab, if he was who he'd said he was, must consider Bill a rival, could have arranged the whole ball to find an opening to the unfathomable Bill. He might, like many others before him, think she was it.

Why hadn't she considered this before?

Wait—wait…Had he expressed interest in her before or after she'd told him who she was?

God—why was she wondering? It wasn't as if *her* identity was a secret. He could have come to the ball knowing all about her. Then she'd gone and given him the best opening to get her alone, to work his magic on her. It wouldn't be the first or last time a man tried to seduce her to get to Bill.

But the glimpse of harshness she'd seen in his eyes…

Oh, God—it could be even worse. He could just be an all-powerful and jaded predator who liked to seduce and abuse women. But she'd thrown herself in his trap too easily, depriving him of the thrill of the hunt and he hadn't wanted to act out his plans for her until he had her totally at his mercy…

He turned unfathomable eyes to her and she felt all her doubts congeal into ugly reality.

Whatever he was, whatever he intended, none of the past hours had been real. None of it had been for her.

How could she have thought he wanted her? No one ever had. How could she have thought he, of all people, could be at the mercy of such a brutal attraction as hers was to him?

Misery engulfed her whole. But she couldn't succumb to it now. Whatever she did, she had to be very careful. She couldn't let her suspicions show. At best she could corner him into an admission, make him turn nasty. At worst she could enrage him, make him show her his true face, make him—make him…

One cabled arm went around her shoulder, pulling her into his hardness and heat, his other hand gentleness itself as he cupped her face and turned it up to him, his eyes blazing with desire once again.

And she couldn't *bear* it.

All her resolutions crumpled and she blurted out, "Please, stop. Whatever you want with me, please, just tell me what it is and get it over with."

Four

Shehab stiffened at Farah's words.

They could only have one meaning.

She'd realized he was playing her.

How had she suspected? He was certain he'd done nothing to give himself away. So what was it? Intuition? Or was she playing a counter-game of her own? If so, to what end? To have him on the defensive, ready to do anything to negate her accusation, tipping the balance of power in her favor?

But she was trembling in his arms, her eyes brimming with tears again, her breathing so erratic it made her breasts shudder against his chest. Not that she seemed aware of this, or the effect it was having on him even now.

Was she that good an actress? He'd known the best virtuoso improvisers and situation analysts who played out impromptu roles wholeheartedly. But he'd always had an infallible detector for insincerity. He sensed none from her now.

Whatever this was, it had struck him from a blind spot. He had to tread with extreme caution until he figured out what was going on. He must maintain the ground he'd won.

To do that, he couldn't pressure her. Even if every instinct was telling him to crush her in his arms and kiss her until she was incoherent with need again.

He took his hands away from her, unbuckled his seat belt, rose to his feet. He struggled to empty his eyes of urgency, to infuse them with all the gentleness he could muster. "Farah, *ya azeezati*—my dear, I don't understand anything. What's wrong?"

"Please, stop acting." She slumped forward, her spun-silk hair and hands hiding her face, her voice thickening with emotion. "I can take anything but that…"

He was at a loss. She knew he was acting. But he wasn't, not when it came to wanting her. So what did she sense? Could she be so sensitive she could feel beyond his raging desire for her to his basic agenda?

It didn't matter what she felt or how she'd come to feel it. Whatever it was, he had to divert her, lull her again.

"And I can take anything but your anguish," he groaned, no longer knowing if his agitation was feigned or real. "Farah, *B'Ellahi,* mere minutes ago you were as elated as I was at being together and now… *Arjooki*—please tell me what went wrong."

She raised streaming eyes, slamming into him with the force of a gut punch. "Everything. I *saw* it."

His hand went to his midriff as if to ward off the pain. But he couldn't afford to let go of her gaze. It would be like admitting his guilt.

He held out against the power of her hurt and accusation, groaned again, "Saw what?"

"Your face, your eyes, filling with…intent, harshness…I don't know." She shook her head, her hair undulating her confusion around her shaking shoulders. "But you're not 'elated' to be with me. You don't want me…you're just like everyone else. No one ever wanted me for me. Or—or it's even worse…"

What *had* she seen? A stray self-congratulatory thought when he'd been prematurely celebrating his triumph?

Fool. He shouldn't even think anything of the sort before he had her signature on all binding documents.

But her distress felt real. So was that the origin of her cold-as-ice, hot-as-hell persona? Not that he'd seen any evidence of her cold side himself, but he could see how she could have been pursued for all the wrong reasons. Sport, ambition, competition, all forms of exploitation. Had the incident he'd manufactured unsettled her so much that it brought back every unsavory situation she'd ever been exposed to, painting *their* situation, and him, with the brush of suspicion? Or had it only sharpened her hazy senses so that she felt he was pursuing her for reasons unconnected with her own desirability?

Suddenly he was sick of the whole thing. If her reputation had been unearned, as everything he'd felt from her so far kept insisting, if she'd been hurt by men's perfidy before, he shouldn't add to her injuries.

But what could he possibly do now? Confess his plan? He'd stood a chance of a favorable response if he'd told her who he was at the beginning. He would have at least gotten points for truthfulness. But he'd been so ready for deception as a necessity for success, he'd lost that chance. After all that had happened between them, all the lies he'd told her, she'd be incensed, might reject him with no hope of reconciliation.

What would he do if she did, when he couldn't let her go? Kidnap her as she'd implied was one of the possibilities he'd seduced her for? Then what? Hold her hostage? Force her to marry him?

Just the thought that things could go so far had bile rising in his throat. He had to stop the situation from spiraling out of control. And he had only one way out.

She'd accused him of not wanting her for herself. *That* he could contest vehemently and sound sincere. For he was.

"You're so wrong I would laugh if this wasn't so distressing. I want you, Farah. I've never wanted anything or anyone like I want you." He took a step toward her and she flinched. He flinched, too, stopped. "*Ya Ullah,* are you afraid of me?" Her eyes closed on a look of total confusion. And he rasped, "Am I paying the price for all of the people who tried to take advantage of you? But as you said, it's even worse. I doubt you actually feared any of them."

Her face contorted on emotions so clear it felt as if she'd shouted them in his mind. Mortification ruled them all.

But her tears were stopping. Then she hiccupped. "It was just-just—finding the plane taking off, that look on your face— and I scared myself with my own speculations..." She paused, gave him a hesitant, vulnerable look. "Do you really want me?"

He drove his hands in his hair in frustration he had no need to feign. "Can't you feel it, in your every cell, setting your senses on fire, how much I desire you?"

She nodded, shook her head, at a total loss. "I do—but I felt...something deeper. If you have any hidden agenda besides..."

He wanted to swear to her that he didn't. He couldn't. The lie clogged in his throat. But he had to defuse her doubts. He must. His only recourse was to reach for whatever truths existed between the lies, press those home to her.

He came down beside her, reached for her restless hands, found them freezing in sweat. He exerted enough pressure to beseech her not to pull them away, while letting her feel she could if she wanted, his eyes soothing her with all his will.

"Every word I told you about how much I desire you is the truth, Farah. And I can't bear to see you in this condition, to know that I'm the reason for it."

She shook her head again. "You're not, it was me."

"It *was* me." He smoothed a glossy lock of hair away from her cheek. "I should have realized how this situation would be overwhelming for you. You were shaken from all that had happened in the past hours, our meeting, our surrender to what you so aptly called 'magic' followed by the paparazzi's intrusion and our escape from them. But instead of giving you time to catch your breath, I whisked you onboard my jet, where you found yourself surrounded by two dozen strange men, most of them armed, as you must have sensed. Then, without even consulting you, I ordered takeoff. You thought we'd have dinner onboard on the ground, didn't you?"

Her eyes said she hadn't thought at all. He caressed her cheek, almost moaning at its firm softness. "You haven't even thought what would happen, and you found yourself receding from your world. Then I added insult to injury when the takeoff had my mind straying to a precarious deal I'm involved in at the moment, giving you a glimpse of the ruthless businessman side of me. It's no wonder you leaped to conclusions."

She winced, bit her lip. Then she finally quavered, "Can you order us to land, please?"

His every muscle clenched. "You don't believe me."

"I do," she protested. Then she pulled an adorably sheepish face. "I just need to be on the ground so I can dig a hole deep enough never to be seen again."

He exhaled the breath that had been about to burst his lungs. But he wouldn't let his guard down again. He'd averted a catastrophe this time. He couldn't let another brew.

He moved closer, still testing. She melted against him and he inhaled with the reprieve. "Don't feel embarrassed by your fears, *ya saherati.* You had every right to wonder, to worry. In fact, I'm almost upset with you for not being more stringent in your examination of my character and intentions before you put yourself in my power this way. You know, like you were cross with me for trusting you based on such a short acquaintance. But then, I believe you wouldn't have done that with anyone else, that you instinctively felt that you have more power over me than you could ever hand me over you."

Farah closed her eyes, shutting out the sight of him, wishing she'd blip out of existence.

She'd made a mess of things. And he was letting her off the hook, exonerating her of all blame, shouldering it all himself.

But she couldn't believe he wasn't offended for real. She was used to being maligned by strangers, by public opinion, but if someone she cared anything for jumped to such unfounded and offensive conclusions about her, she wouldn't be quick to forgive and forget. Could it be true he did so completely?

She opened her eyes, found anxiety still tingeing his gaze.

He had. And more. He felt horrible about his alleged role in her out-of-the-blue upheaval. He'd come up with explanations that saved her from looking like an irrational airhead. She felt herself shrink to the size and significance of a bug.

She pressed her face into his hand. "Please, stop being so gallant and understanding or no hole will be deep enough."

She felt like whooping when his lips twitched. "I can see this developing into a loop, with me saying I did it and you saying, no, I did. So how about we let our feelings of guilt cancel out each other and get on with our enchanted evening?"

"Why would you want to spend more time with a moron who more or less accused you of being a fraud or even a criminal?"

"I can wonder why you would want to spend more time with

a lout who didn't even ask your permission before taking you out of your national airspace. But I won't. We agreed to think the best of each other's actions and motivations."

She gave him a sardonic look. "I didn't agree to anything. But you're used to this, aren't you? You announce stuff and assume everyone's in agreement with it."

"See?" His eyes crinkled. "I did it again. You've uncovered my biggest vice. I'm part bulldozer."

She gave in to the urge, ran a finger down a slashed cheekbone. "Only part? And that's your biggest vice? You sure there aren't bigger ones?"

"As much as I'd love to have you take my character apart and haul out vices for examination, we have more pressing issues to worry about now. Like food. Didn't you work up an appetite after all the upheavals? I ordered my chef to prepare my favorite dishes from my country's cuisine for you to sample."

The way he said that, and in his mouth-watering voice, too, made her stomach grumble.

His lips spread wide. "I guess I have my answer."

He pushed more buttons. In minutes he opened the door to a parade of waiters holding their trays high. Even under covers, aromas emanated from the dishes that had her licking her lips.

He rose to his feet, held out his hand. She took it, let him pull her to her feet. Before she fell against him, he pulled back, his eyes once more becoming unfathomable. This time the only alarm she felt was that she might have, in spite of his assurances, introduced distance between them.

He led her behind the screen to a dining area with stainless steel–backed, burgundy velvet-upholstered chairs and a Plexiglas table for two laid out in stunning hand-painted china, silver, crystal and burgundy silk.

As soon as the last waiter had departed, Shehab raised a

silver dome off a service plate. The sight and aroma hit her senses in unison.

At her moan he said, "This is *matazeez*—veal cubes cooked in tomato sauce before adding okra, aubergine and zucchini. The stuff that looks like ravioli is specially prepared dough that's rolled out and cut and dropped in the mix before it's fully cooked so that it retains its chewiness. Some people consider this a full meal, some eat it with rice or *khobez*."

"That's this bread?" He nodded, and as she bent for a closer sniff, his smile grew as hot as the dish simmering on the flames. "Who would have guessed you'd know so much about the preparation of the dishes you love."

"You didn't think it possible for me to know how to cook?"

"If you do, I'll know you're a hallucination."

He chuckled as he pushed a button, made a chair retract from the table on rails embedded in the fuselage.

She flopped into it, groaned. "Don't describe any more dishes. Just looking at them and smelling them was making my stomach lick its lips, but your descriptions are making it grow forks and knives." He laughed. She moaned. At the sound. At the scents of food mixed with that of virility.

He served her a portion, but when she tried to reach for a real fork and knife, he stopped her, sat and maneuvered the opposing chair until it touched hers, picked up a fork and started feeding her, all the time caressing her with his eyes.

And what could she do but wallow in the incredible experience of being waited on, fed, by this god?

She demolished the portion in minutes, exclaiming at the taste and texture, participating in his quiz of guessing the elusive seasonings, correctly identifying cinnamon and nutmeg. That very distinctive spice turned out to be something she'd never heard about before, *semmaq*, a spice unique to his region.

At some point, he started alternating forkfuls between them, and sharing the meal with him that way surpassed even the intimacy of the frenzied time they'd shared in the gardens.

When he started feeding her dessert, she moaned. "*This* I have to ask about. You can resume your recipe description."

He chuckled. "That's *maasoob.* It's *khobez,* cut into small pieces, fried crispy, mashed with banana and brown sugar and caramelized in butter. The sprinkling on top is paprika, saffron and the tasty black seeds are *hab el barakah,* literally, blessing seeds."

She moaned again as the sinful concoction slid on her tongue and down her throat. "Blessing or curse? My hips and thighs are already screaming the latter."

"Those are a blessing unto themselves. A little more of them would be a bigger blessing."

"Oh, no. I struggled long and hard with my weight as I grew up and I'm never going back there."

He put the spoon down, his eyes a heavy caress over her body. "I wanted you to sample the richness of the flavors of my culture, but if this perfection is a result of your hard work, I certainly won't do anything to sabotage it."

A tightness clutched her throat. Whenever she'd made a statement like that in the past, everyone had scoffed at her with reactions ranging from disbelief that she had such concerns, to accusing her of fishing for compliments, to choosing to believe she'd just been blessed with a nuclear metabolism and could gorge herself on junk constantly and not gain an ounce.

But he understood. And supported. He was just phenomenal.

And he was on his feet, inviting her to leave the table.

She let him lead her back to the lounge, where he took her to a different seating area, this time sitting on an armchair across from her. She watched him, obsessing over his every detail.

He watched her examining his every inch for a long moment,

then he suddenly said, "It just came to me, one more thing that I think caused your alarm. The man you trusted and wanted was the man you saw in the *Tuareg* garb. Seeing me in these clothes must have made you feel as if I were someone else."

Her eyes jerked up from watching the ripple of steel muscles below the fine cloth of his pants. "This—uh, *Tuareg* garb is how you usually dress in your country?"

"Hardly. *Tuaregs* come from and still live mostly in the North African desert and are quite proud of the purity of their lineage. My ancestors, who come from all over Asia wouldn't have been allowed within a mile of marriage into their tribes."

"God, I must sound so ignorant, assuming all Arabs have the same origins."

The teasing in his eyes intensified. "Tuaregs can't be called Arabs. They call themselves *Kel Tamajag,* or Speakers of Tamasheq, a language that has nothing in common with Arabic. But it's understandable that you might lump peoples who hail from a general direction into one basket. Back home, a lot of people consider all white people 'Americans.'"

"I'm sure that's not true of those above a certain education level. People with my education anywhere in the world have no excuse for being so oblivious and making such generalizations. I'm lamentably ignorant about your part of the world."

"I will teach you. Everything you want to know."

And she'd bet he didn't mean only about the complexities of his region and its various cultures and peoples.

She groped for breath. "OK, you can start now. What do you wear where you come from?"

"Most men wear white *taub* and *ghotrah* or red-and-white-checkered *shmagh* with black *eggal* headdress. They add a black *abaya* if it gets cold. I wear modern clothes, except in formal functions. Sorry to disappoint you, but I don't always go around looking like I've just stepped out of *Arabian Nights*."

"It does disappoint me." And she *had* to tell him that? Then she told him more. "Which is weird, really. I've never much cared for that kind of getup, or even seen the *Arabian Nights* connection. But then, I've never seen *you* in one…"

It was hopeless. She was doomed to tell him everything just as it formed in her mind. She just prayed it didn't put him off.

He seemed anything but put off as his eyes devoured her. "*Ya gummari*, I have an extensive wardrobe right out of my culture's rich past and I'll dress up in whatever takes your fancy. I bet I'll learn to love these intricate outfits when you're undressing me, layer by layer…" Then he sighed. "Until then, I must settle for fantasies and anticipation."

Blood shot to her face before splashing through her body.

He shook his head as he took in her condition. "Hours ago you were ready to let me make love to you, and now you're blushing to your toes at my mildly erotic innuendoes?"

"Mildly? Yeah, right. But that aside, wouldn't you be embarrassed out of your skin if it was sinking in that you'd almost done something so out of character with a virtual stranger, and but for his clout, it would have been plastered all over the tabloids for the world to see?"

"Don't you think 'out of character' is too mild a description for anything I'd do if the stranger were of the 'his' variety?"

She glared at him. "You're laughing at me!"

His shook his head again. "*With* you."

It didn't placate her. Her brain felt scrambled, would remain so as long as he kept "…*making me make a fool of myself.*"

Shehab watched her in rising confusion.

Was she telling him she didn't go for sex with strangers?

Didn't indulge in one-night stands? Or literally few-minutes stands, as she'd begged him to be?

The last of the ease in her pose, the softness in her lips and the dreaminess in her eyes evaporated. "Sorry I said that out loud. No one makes you do anything you don't want to. I made a fool of myself and I got caught. And I have to face the music sooner or later. So, listen, when we land, forget about what I said about going to a hotel. I'll take a taxi home, get it over with."

For some reason the spell kept being interrupted and this unpredictable woman kept swinging between opposites while he was left reeling. First the uncharted reaction to the paparazzi, then that empathic episode. And now. What was it now? Was she coming to her senses, envisioning possible damages from their liaison?

But if she was, why wasn't she trying to get away with it? So far there was no incriminating evidence against her.

Had she decided he wasn't worth the trouble of risking anything further? Was she cutting him off?

"You promised to see me again, and again."

"Yeah, that was before I remembered I was a paparazzi magnet. And I can't let you be plastered all over the tabloids."

Was this just an excuse to get rid of him? Or could it be she was really worried about causing him a scandal? Her words did have the inimitable ring of truth to them. Not that, after tonight, he'd recognize the truth if it punched him in the gut.

"You're concerned for my privacy?"

"It takes one who has none to know how valuable it is. You've been very wise to keep your anonymity. Nothing is worth endangering that."

"You are. Worth that, and far more."

She winced. "Don't exaggerate, please. You barely know me. How do you know what I'm worth? And from the way I behaved with you so far, I know any man would be thinking I'm not worth much. But you of all men… So I believe you want me, but I'd hate to peek inside your head and read what you really think of me."

"I, of all men? What's so different about me?"

"What's *not* different about you? And then, you come from a culture that glorifies feminine modesty and virtue, and is cruel to women who don't abide by its strict rules, and I—I…"

"Your mind is taking off on tangents again. You're punishing yourself for a nonexistent misdemeanor. I don't believe so-called virtue is required of women any more than it is of men. Do you consider me to be a degenerate for letting our first encounter take an erotic turn that fast?"

"You know I don't. It was you who stopped, you who had control over yourself, while I—I…"

"You were over your head."

She nodded, her eyes downcast.

"I was, too. The one thing that made me stop was my fear of this exact situation, after your blood cooled and you couldn't defend your actions to yourself, driving you to push me away in shame and discomfort at what you consider a lapse."

"I didn't say it was a lapse. I said it was out of character. So much so, I don't know how to handle it, don't know what to think…"

"Well, I do. I think I've never known desire like that existed. But it *is* so pure, so powerful I don't know how to handle it, either. The one thing I could think to do was to slow down, savor it…savor you. Though you're making it almost impossible to do that. Everything you say, every breath you draw is making me want to unwrap you and swallow you whole."

Her color brightened, her gaze wavered. "Are you sure seeing me again won't jeopardize your privacy? I'm overexposed and quite often maligned, and it would be awful if any of the venom I inspire from the media spilled into your life. I can't let it."

He was suddenly incensed. With the people who caused such upheaval in her life. With himself for ever devising the plan that had injured her so much. That could end with him losing her.

He rose from his armchair and joined her on the couch. "The paparazzi can't touch me," he bit off. "And I will convince them to collectively forget you ever existed."

She blinked at his ferocity. Then she did another totally unexpected thing. She giggled. "I assume you'd use methods harsher than what's fully sanctioned by the law to obtain this miraculous result?"

"I wouldn't be doing anything they didn't richly deserve," he rumbled. "Breeching others' privacy, shattering their peace."

"You come from a culture that advocates an eye for an eye, don't you? Uh…there I go, putting my foot in it again…"

"Never worry about saying anything to me. I have no sensitivities for you to tread on. Even if I did, you shouldn't censor your words, anyway. I think political correctness is becoming reverse persecution, and I refuse to bow to its unreasonable demands. Anyway, you're right about my culture, and me, advocating an eye for an eye. But I believe the rest of this decree is the relevant part. The aggressor is to blame."

Her smile died as she digested his words. He was thankful to note that her agitation hadn't returned with the dimming.

Then she sighed. "God, that's tempting. But now that I realize what kind of power your possess, I can't use it for my own ends. With great power comes great responsibility and all that. I'd feel I was nuking someone for spitting in my face. No, leave them be. They'll get bored with me sooner or later."

"You'd be that merciful when they've shown you no mercy? When they make their livelihood by preying on your life?"

"I don't know about merciful. I just can't be party to the

ugliness they propagate, and by retaliating I'd just be poisoning the world more, not to mention muddying my own karma."

He clamped his jaw on the need to pulverize her reticence, wanting her to give him carte blanche to remove the vultures from her path once and for all.

He wrestled the urge down, if only by coming to a decision that he *would* do it, if with less-than-harsh methods to honor her choice. He still couldn't stop himself from saying, "I will keep on hoping that you'll change your mind, let me use my…discretion in dealing with them. Until then, they're coming nowhere near you. We won't go back to your home. And I certainly won't take you to a hotel. Come be with me, *ya jameelati.*"

After a stunned moment, she stammered, "I know I gave you the impression—hell, I *asked* you to—to…but I really am out of my depth here, Shehab."

"I'm not asking you to come to my place to share my bed. I said we'd go slow, and we will, as slow as we need to. I'm offering my protection and hospitality as long as you need it."

"Oh, God, Shehab, I don't think…"

"How about you stop thinking for a while?"

She squeezed her eyes shut. "But that's the problem. I stopped thinking at all since I met you."

His fingers feathered her eyes open. "And why is that such a bad thing? The past hours have been a roller coaster. Take the next, and all the time you stay at my place, to settle down, relax, enjoy my company, savor me as I intend to savor you."

"But I have to…to…I don't know what I have to do, OK? Whatever it is, I can't do it with you around. Please, Shehab, just take me home. I need to wrap my head around tonight, around what happened between us, the way I—I…"

And she fell silent.

He was losing her. She was coming to her senses. He couldn't afford to let her. He had to move into a higher gear.

He slipped his cell phone out of his pocket, gave a twofold order. The first part was another improvisation in his plan. He told her the second part. "I ordered the plane to land."

She nodded, looked anywhere but at him. He put the phone on the couch between them, gritted his teeth and counted down…

A buzz went through her. It took her seconds to realize it wasn't another jolt of awareness. It was his phone's vibration.

He answered it unhurriedly, his eyes on her.

After the first seconds his eyes shifted away and his face closed. Her heart contracted. Bad news? Personal?

He bit off a string of Arabic before he snapped the phone shut. She watched him with a thudding heart as he placed it on the table before them, his moves deliberate, as if to delay a reaction to something big. And bad.

Then he finally sought her eyes and her heart lurched. "An unforeseen crisis has blown apart the business deal I mentioned earlier."

She stared at him, held her breath, hoping he'd elaborate. Next second she wished she hadn't hoped. She should have known whatever she hoped for would happen in reverse.

He went on. "I can't predict how long it will take to perform damage control, to reestablish matters. Weeks. Maybe months."

"Oh." That was all she could say.

What was there to say when he was telling her it had been too good to go any further? He'd go back home, for weeks, maybe months. And he'd forget all about her.

It was over before it had even begun.

Five

"So—this is goodbye?"

Farah heard the disembodied voice. It was hers.

Shehab looked away, his face an empty mask now. "I guess it is." After a moment's crushing silence he added, "I would have asked to see you after I've dealt with the crisis, but I guess there's no point anymore."

Her heart twisted. So she'd still been hoping that he'd contest her verdict. But he was too truthful to say something he didn't mean, even for courtesy's sake. He knew he'd forget her in that time, probably thought it would be good riddance anyway.

But what had she expected? Her behavior might have intrigued him at first, or at least entertained him. But after her candidness and abandon had turned to agitation and accusation, after she'd behaved like an insecure fool wrapped in a moronic virgin following her impression of a nymphomaniac hours ago, too, it must have been a major turnoff to him, a man of a level of sophistication and self-possession she hadn't dreamed existed.

But he'd still been so accommodating, so patient, had tried to talk her down from her unreasonable state, tolerated her yo-yoing moods, up until she'd turned down his offer of sanctuary.

She'd wanted to hide until she came to terms with what he'd made her feel, want, do. But she hadn't turned down his offer, had only been postponing accepting until she was ready.

She'd thought she'd be ready tomorrow.

Now there would be no tomorrow. Now she would have nothing. Nothing but the memories of this unbelievable man and night. And the discoveries about herself she'd been merci-fully oblivious to. At least her previous resignation to her status quo, her ignorance of what she was capable of feeling had re-sembled peace.

But as usual, she had no say in anything. He'd disappear from her life and she couldn't do anything about it.

There was one thing she *could* do, though. Give him his dues, tell him how she wished she'd used their precious time better and given him as fond memories of her as he'd given her of him.

"Shehab, I want to tell you how sorry I am, for everything—" He raised one hand in a cutting gesture. "OK, so you don't want to hear it, but I have to say it. You gave me a night out of time, one nothing will ever come close to touching in my life, and I gave you only a headache in return."

He snapped his eyes back to her then, the harshness there directed at her, no doubt. "You've been so incredibly candid so far, so please, don't *you* start acting now."

"Acting?"

"Yes, to assume the blame for how things have turned out, so you'll soften the blow. I won't pretend it is a disappointment I can come to terms with, as it isn't and I can't. But please don't add insult to injury and think you need to placate me now. It's your right to change your mind at any point."

"You're the one who changed your mind." Her voice quavered.

He shot to his feet. "I did no such thing."

"But you said there was no point in looking me up anymore."

"Only because you've made it clear you don't want to see me. And since you seem horrified by what you let happen between us, after your earlier doubts, I don't want to give them credence by imposing my desire where it isn't wanted, adding the charges of stalking and harassment to…" He stopped, stared at her as she gaped at him. Then his stiff face broke into slow elation that made her feel like the sun had broken through barricades of clotted clouds and a heavenly orchestra had broken out to fill the world with poignancy and beauty. "You *weren't* telling me you didn't want to see me again?"

"If I in any way implied that, then my communication skills, as stunted as they are, have totally disintegrated."

Something tight, watchful, still hovered in his gaze. "But you said you wanted to go home."

"I only wanted to go home tonight. I was hoping to be with you again tomorrow, when I hoped also to have retrieved my misplaced balance and borrowed some much-needed discretion."

And the tension in his eyes, his stance, disappeared as he leaned closer until he had her imprisoned between his arms, lowered his head to hers until his breath singed her cheek, her jaw. "I pray no one ever lends you any. In fact, I'll do whatever it takes to ensure no one does. You captivate me with your frankness, you elate me with your spontaneity."

She sounded as if she'd sprinted a mile as she said, "Even when they took a turn into frank and spontaneous paranoia?"

He raised his face. "I would bear anything to have them. But I'd also do anything never to have you flinch away from me or see pain and doubt fill your eyes again."

"Oh, I'll never do that again. And you'll never see those—" she gulped as she realized how stupid that sounded, how futile "—for the whole whopping hour I have left in your company."

He took her by the shoulders, his eyes brooking no argument. "But I will see you again. When this crisis is over."

"Yeah, sure."

He came down beside her again, turned her to him. "What does your sarcasm signify here, *ya jameelati?*"

"Just that in a few months you probably won't remember meeting me, let alone take the trouble to come and see me again."

He shook his head. "How can you underestimate your effect on me to that extent? You think I'd forget you?" He clamped her shoulders again, his eyes filling with what looked like a vow. "These months away from you will be like serving a sentence. I'll count down each minute until I can come to you again."

Her heart ricocheted inside her like a released balloon, before it dropped into her gut, deflated and limp. "Oh, Shehab, that's exactly how I feel." Her breath caught at the flare in his eyes. She smoothed his formidable jaw, attempted a smile that trembled apart. "But if you come back, I won't mind."

He pressed his hand over hers, making her cup his face. "Then you're far stronger than I. I will go mad with frustration and probably let what I'm leaving you to handle go to hell."

Her heart zoomed at the passion in his face, the conviction in his voice, before it sputtered at his meaning.

"No, you won't." Her other hand came up, cradling his face in an attempt to soothe him as he had her, so many times this tempestuous night. "So many people count on you, and you'll resolve everything with a flick of a hand as you always do. And while you're away, we don't have to be cut off from one another, do we? We can phone, e-mail, have video-conferencing…"

"And make the longing even more insupportable."

She choked on the truth of his words, nodded miserably. "I already miss you and you're still right here."

Then she was in his arms, every part of her exposed flesh covered in a fever of kisses. She was shaking apart when he wrenched his lips away. "This is once in a lifetime, and I can't leave it—can't leave *you* behind. Come with me, *ya* Farah."

She jerked. "C-come with you? How?"

His lips curled at her squeak. "I will order my pilots to gain altitude again and chart a course for my home."

She struggled out of his embrace, scampered up to her knees on the couch, glared down on him. "*Now* you're laughing at me."

He sat up, took her face in both his hands. "I've never felt less humorous in my life. I mean it, Farah. Come with me."

She sagged in his hold again with the blow of sheer nerve-racking disbelief. He was offering her a continuation, a chance to be with him. Really *with* him. In his home…

But… "How? And don't you dare describe the flight plan. You have a crisis on your hands…"

"Let me worry about that."

She barely heard him, barreled on. "And I have work…"

One hand covered her mouth, gentle, inexorable, suspending all words, all thought. Then he commanded, "Take a vacation."

Shehab watched stupefaction follow the parade of emotions spilling all over Farah's face. It was as if he'd proposed she should fly. Under her own power.

Sure enough, she mumbled into his hand, "I don't take vacations."

He'd had reports of how she was always present at work. He'd thought her lover was keeping her on a short leash. But now it seemed it was she who'd never considered taking time off.

He removed his hand, stroked her cheek. "Never?"

She looked as if realization had just dawned on her. "Guess I never had anything to do with my free time, so I never wanted it."

"Don't you want it now? To be with me?" Her eyes blazed with such blatant admission that he groaned. "If you come with me, I'll commute to and from the locations I need to be in and come back to you every available minute of each day."

"You really want this, want me to go home with you, back to—to…" She stopped, almost panting. "Where do you live, anyway?"

"I live on an island off the coast of Damhoor." He didn't mention that the closest shores where those of Judar. He didn't want to bring up the place he didn't want her to associate him with. And he was counting on that ignorance she'd confessed. She hadn't even bothered to look up her biological father's kingdom on a map. If she had, she'd have learned that Zohayd wasn't only Judar's neighbor, but Damhoor's, too. And she might have grown uncomfortable. As it was, the only agitation he felt from her was shock clashing with elation and indecision. He had to pulverize the latter, fast. He knew the best way to do that.

He let his eyes grow heavy with feigned pain. "You still don't trust me, Farah?"

This provoked the response he'd been counting on. A vehement… "*No*. It's just so sudden, so—so huge, so wonderful an offer, and on top of everything that happened tonight, I'm not just out of my depth, I'm up in the air…uh, in every way possible."

He smiled down on her. This was working. He'd fulfill his prophecy, savoring her at leisure. He could almost taste it.

He took a taste of her now. "Say yes, Farah."

She melted into him, offering her lips for him to consume, her every muscle and bone saying yes, yes, yes for her.

When he withdrew to let her make her consent verbal, she gasped, "But I still have to go back home…"

"No, you don't, *ya gummari*."

"But I need to change—this dress is fused to my skin, and—man, as if this is even worth mentioning. I need to pack the important stuff. All I have on me are my keys. Right now I'm no one, with no money or passport or even a toothbrush…"

He swallowed her babbling in another clinging kiss. "Is this a yes?"

She hissed the pleasure-laden word of capitulation into his mouth. *"Yes."*

He took his fill for as long as he dared to, then pulled back, triumph roaring in his system. "Though I'll be sorry to say goodbye to this dress, you can change out of it right now. I let my sister use the jet on her trips to and from the States—she's doing her Master's and spreading her wings—and she leaves clothes onboard." He took another taste of those flushed lips as if compelled. "Let's see, what's left? A toothbrush. You'll have a dozen to choose from in a minute. A new passport will be waiting for you when we arrive, as well as anything you can want or need. Then we can fly into Damhoor or Bidalya if you need to pick anything yourself."

"But I don't have money…oh, OK, now I know what tossed salad feels like. Can't believe I worried about that." So she remembered she'd be his guest, fully subsidized, of course. "It'll take a couple of days to get new credit cards issued." That was what she'd meant? She didn't expect him to spend money on her? Suddenly her eyes rounded. "Scratch tossed salad. My brain's milkshake. I'm bringing up credit cards and toothbrushes and not arranging for my absence at work!"

He withdrew, offered her his phone. "Then go ahead."

She shook her head, sat up, looking around for her purse. He retrieved it for her before he sat down across from her again. She got out her own phone with unsteady fingers, pushed a speed-dial button.

In seconds she said, "Bill, it's me. No, nothing's wrong…" She paused as the rancorous grumbling of a bear with a sore paw rumbled on the other end. "Sorry for waking you up. 5:00 a.m.?" Her eyes shot up to him, wide with disbelief. "I—I didn't realize it was that late." Another pause. "Yeah, I left the ball early. You didn't make it at all, huh? Listen, Bill, I'll just say this and let you get back to sleep. I won't be coming to work tomorrow— uh, make that today. No—I'm not ill. Since when do I take days off when I'm ill?" A longer pause. "Bill, I'm not taking a day off, I'm taking a vacation."

She paused, waiting for Bill to say something. Seemed he was too stunned to respond. She went on. "It just came to me that it's been seven years since I came to work for you, so we can call this a sabbatical, really. But don't worry, everything's in order, and I'm a phone call away if you need to ask me anything. I'll also have an Internet connection…" She looked at him. He gave an "of course" gesture. "So just e-mail me with urgent stuff."

A torrent exploded on the other end. She made the face of someone being forced to listen to a thousand nails scratching on a board. At last she interrupted. "I did give you every reason to believe I'm some sort of an android, but look up my contract and you'll find out I do belong to the race with those pesky little side benefits called human rights. And of course there is the job description, which we both know I've gone far and above beyond." She fell silent again, but Bill had been duly chastised and spoke now at a volume that didn't carry beyond the phone's receiver. "Yeah, it is overdue. Uh, I don't know how long it'll be…" She again looked at him. He shook his head, catching his lower lip on the sensuality of open-ended promise. It would be as long as it took to make her an Aal Masood bride. She smiled back, hunger glowing in her eyes before Bill drew her back to their conversation. She smiled again, affectionately this time. "And you take care of yourself." She lowered her voice and averted her face, smiling as she murmured, "I'll miss you, too."

Shehab felt as if a stinging slap had landed on his cheek.

And every preconceived opinion of her crashed back on him, blasting away her spell, jogging him back to ugly reality.

Here she was, the woman who'd treated him to such a kaleidoscope of emotions for the past ten hours, sitting before him, her future lover, talking to her current one, lying to him, to them both, without batting a lid.

She slid shut her phone and looked at him, elation sizzling in her eyes, looking like a little girl who'd just done something naughty for the first time in her life.

He struggled to empty his gaze of aggression, to access the desire that was independent of his opinion of her. He felt it only becoming fiercer without the shackles of softness, the brakes of empathy, until he struggled not to rise and pounce on her. He had no idea how he only smiled, opened his arms wide.

She rose and rushed to throw herself into them, all fairy-tale gown, overpowering femininity and undetectable pretense. But one thing she wasn't pretending about.

She couldn't wait for him.

He'd make her wait. And when the time was right, he'd end the waiting. He'd sate himself with her. Then, when she'd served her purpose, even as they continued their sham of a marriage, he'd discard her. And he wouldn't feel bad about it.

She deserved whatever he did to her.

Shehab was doing things to Farah she hadn't known there were to be done.

All through their flight, he'd proved to her there was no ceiling to the sensations he could make her experience.

He was now examining her hand as they talked. Shaping each

finger with his fingertips, sliding up and down their length, following the outline of each bone and joint, mapping the pattern of each crease and line, testing the resilience of each pad of flesh. She lay back, enveloped in his sister's cool, white cotton sundress, drenched in the cold sweat of stimulation, tormented, hypersensitive and praying that he'd never stop exposing her to his attention and appreciation.

Suddenly she interrupted his account about the neighboring Damhoor. "I had no idea hands could be erogenous zones..."

She started to bite her lip, stopped, sighed. They'd been talking almost nonstop for the past twenty hours, all but for the half hour she'd left to change and shower, followed by two separate half hours when he'd left her to do the same and then take care of other details. He was beyond certain by now that she had no filtering system in her brain to stop inappropriate comments from gushing through uncensored—and he kept assuring her he loved it.

His smile knocked her breath from her. Ever since she'd accepted his invitation to go home with him, she'd sensed some change in him. A new intensity. As if he'd been holding back and had let go. It had worried her. For about a nanosecond.

She trusted him, wanted him to feel as intensely about her as she did about him. And his intensity had so many levels and textures, it felt like a deep ocean she could plunge into forever, exploring and experiencing, and never come close to fathoming.

"And I had no idea just holding your hands could awaken new erogenous areas, in both my body and brain." Her heat shot up another notch at his confession. She was already addicted to how open he was about his feelings, too. He took her hand to his lips, flicked his tongue lightly along her lifeline. She hoped he wasn't shortening said life's expectancy. He had her squirming before he withdrew. "And by the way, we've arrived."

She twisted around to peer out the window. They were descending, approaching his island. It was shaped like an irregular kidney, with its concave side harboring bright emerald waters, its outer curve surrounded by much darker ones. In the noon sun its wraparound beaches shone almost silver, pristine except where mangroves covered them in areas on the convex side. The jet was now flying over one apex of the island, just above a low, huge building that overlooked a bay. Dense palm trees and what looked like all sorts of desert flora surrounded it on three sides. The jet was flying over other annexed structures heading to the other end of the island when it hit her.

She turned to him, exclaimed, "It's a real island."

His smile grew wicked. "That was the general idea when I said it was. You know, land surrounded on all sides by water."

She gave him a playful poke. "So I'm geographically challenged, but not to that extent. I thought it would be one of those tiny morsels of land advertised on the Internet as private islands. But this is just…just wow. How big is it?"

She had no idea why, but her eyes dragged down his body until they stumbled on the bulge in his pants. She snatched them up only to find his gaze had been investigating the path of her fascination before it came up, steamy, challenging.

"How big do you think it is?"

"Big." And there was no doubt what her croaked adjective was referring to, not when her blush must be suffusing the air around her with a reddish glow.

He decided to take pity on her, to pretend they weren't talking about his endowments. "It's around 150 square miles."

"That's more than the combined size of the Maldives!"

"So you're not that geographically challenged after all."

"I only know that because Bill has recently expanded his shipping interests to those islands."

His face remained smiling, but it now felt like the frozen, eerie smile she got when she hit Pause on a video. And again unease slithered down her spine.

This had happened every time she'd mentioned Bill. Could he have heard that Bill had a younger mistress, and either realized or suspected it was her? She'd just die if he had.

But he wasn't one to let something like that go unverified. And she was certain he wouldn't come near another man's woman, mistress or whatever.

No. He couldn't know. Thank God. And she would rather skydive without a parachute than explain how this charade—which she intended to end as soon as she saw Bill again—had started.

So what did the stillness that came over him when she mentioned Bill mean? Was the businessman in him shoving aside the passionate man every time anything or anyone connected with business was mentioned?

Whatever it was, she shouldn't try to analyze it. She now recognized that any apprehension she felt originated within her, was triggered by her inability to believe her luck.

She still couldn't hold his gaze, turned away to watch the ground zooming closer. And suddenly realized what else was wrong with this picture. She hadn't thought... "...we'd be landing here!"

His eyebrows rose. "Care to explain that outburst to a poor man whose first language isn't English?"

She groaned. "You'd have to speak Farahish to get it. That's a language half-spoken mentally, with the out-loud half coming out as seemingly out-of-the-blue incoherencies."

His eyes crinkled as he smoothed her cheek with the back of his hand. "I can't tell you how eager I am to be fluent in Farahish. But I think I'm getting the hang of the basics. You didn't think we'd actually land on the island, did you?"

"You understood! Wow. People always think it's a sign of loose brain components, and it only gets worse when I explain."

He frowned. "It's pointless to try to explain anything to those whose minds were poured in casts. But I'm almost grateful to the rigid wretches. They make you appreciate me even more."

"If I appreciated you more than that I'd be in deep d…" She gulped, then stammered, "Uh…anyway—I did have a mental image of a tiny island and assumed we'd land in a neighboring kingdom and head here by a smaller jet, maybe a helicopter or yacht."

They touched down as she spoke, a perfect, imperceptible landing. She was so impressed she broke out clapping.

He laughed. "The pilots can't hear you as they would on a commercial flight, but I'll make sure to relay your approval."

Godly *and* gracious. She beamed at him. "Oh, please do."

He rose to his feet, smiled down on her. "Shall we?"

She jumped up and groaned as everything inside her did, too. His arm came around her, his touch and gaze concerned.

"My joints need oiling after sitting down for so long."

He pinched her cheek softly. "Next time, take my advice. If you'd at least lain down in one of the bedrooms, you wouldn't be aching all over now. But have no fear. All joints will get well oiled around here. You won't sit down much while I'm around."

He let that marinate in her mind with a hundred mental spices as he walked her down through the jet to the air-stairs.

The moment the stairs touched down, hot, dry air rushed in to greet them, making her gasp. He secured her to him as they descended to the tarmac. She smiled up her thankfulness—and gasped again.

If she'd thought seeing Shehab by moonlight had added to his mystique, to his beauty, she'd again been measuring by mere mortals' standards, those who needed darkness to hide their imperfections. In the merciless glare of the island sun, Shehab was—was… There was no single adjective. Not a dozen, either.

Where a twelve-hour beard made most men look unkempt and in need of a shave and shower, it only deepened his bronze statue impression. His skin really was perfect, spread taut over the masterpiece chiseling of his bone structure, burnished, the color so complex, so rich it set off the whites of his eyes, the night of his irises. His hair looked alive, the luxury of its waves an extension of his vigor and character as much as his eyes and lips and hands, its ebony highlighted by honest-to-goodness indigoes and blues as if his electric nature imbued it. And then came his features. She hated to think what the light and the harsh shadows it generated were doing to her own haven't-seen-daylight-in-seven-years paleness. But exposed to their pitiless test, the symmetry and precision of his features were enhanced to the point where she felt she'd discover he was some higher being after all.

Before she could again wonder how such a being could be as hard hit by her as she was by him, he rushed her to a sleek, matte-black monster of a toy, a helicopter the likes of which she'd never seen before.

In moments she was strapped into the passenger seat and he was in the pilot seat and they were sweeping away from the mini-airport in a smooth arc to soar over the sandy and rocky terrain of the mostly virgin island.

"You can fly," she finally exclaimed.

"No, I can't. I can't even manage simple levitation under my own power. But I'm working on it."

She pinched his arm and he threw back his head and laughed. She was becoming addicted to the way he ribbed her, too.

She teased back. "Well, until you manage it and I can pick your brain for the method, will you teach me how to fly this beauty? I always wanted to be able to fly something, but never got the chance to try even a kite."

"I'll teach you to fly, *ya jameelati*. Everything." His eyes became heavy with promise. "And in every way."

With that he left her dealing with another attack of arrhythmia and concentrated on flying, and talking on his radio.

In ten minutes they were approaching the mansion she'd seen from the jet. Then they were landing in a cobblestone courtyard nestled between palm trees at the side facing away from the sea.

He rushed around to hand her down. As soon as she was out of the copter's controlled environment, her feet wobbled.

He swept her up in his arms. "The heat's too much for you?"

Her head flopped on his shoulder. "Now it is." He chuckled, strode toward the mansion, which looked deserted. "But before you had me defying gravity, what got to me was the crisp purity of the air. I feel like a fish out of her AC-grown bacteria and carbon monoxide."

He chuckled again. "Mermaid, not fish. But I'll detox you. This beauty deserves only the best this earth has to offer."

Surprised again by his praise—the one thing that had managed to stun her into silence—she clung to him, took in his mansion.

Built of sandstone and covering at least thirty thousand square feet, it combined the rawness of the natural habitat, the richness of the culture and the grandeur of royal prosperity. As far as she could tell, it had architectural influences from all over Arabia and Asia in its design, in every line, embellishment, column, arch, door and window, but there were also other influences, simpler ones—Bedouin, even a bit of modern. Much like its owner, the mansion was a mix of the best of all worlds. And like him, its overall effect was breathtaking.

As soon as he scaled the dozen stone steps leading to the

columned patio, footmen in Arabian garb seemed to materialize
out of nowhere, rushing to open the gigantic oak double doors.

She blinked at them as Shehab crossed into the darkened
interior. She should have known the deserted impression was an
illusion. A place this big must have dozens of people seeing to its
upkeep. And they'd stay out of the way until Shehab needed them.

Flustered that they'd seen her in Shehab's arms, she tried to
resume autonomy. But he tightened his hold, dropped a kiss on
her temple. "You're exhausted, *ya jameelati*. Let me pamper you."

She went limp in his arms once more, surrendered to his
coddling as the interior's coolness robbed her of what was left
of her volition. He was right. She was exhausted. It had been over
thirty hours since they'd met. It felt like thirty chaotic days.
Weeks. Within ten of those hours, she'd made a decision that
would change her life, change *her,* forever.

As he swept her through his mansion, she barely took in the
gigantic hall in the subdued lighting of a circular bronze chande-
lier that was strung up by dozens of feet of chains from the
soaring ceiling to hang just a few feet above head level. All she
registered acres of sand-colored marble floors and a massive
fountain in the center of it all. As they passed it, the sound of
water made her bones melt faster.

He climbed up one side of the twenty-foot-wide marble stairs
that bifurcated to the upper floor, entered a corridor as wide as
her condo back home. Still holding her securely in one arm, he
opened an arched oak door, entered an expansive bedroom. His?

Her powers of observation were dwindling. She got only impressions of mirrorlike floors, soaring ceilings, whitewashed
walls, ten-foot terrace windows draped in semi-opaque brick-
colored curtains that turned the ambiance inside the room into
that of a warm, intimate dream.

The one thing she saw every detail of was the bed. Huge,

spread in crisp white sheets and an Arabian-design earth-tone bedspread. He swept away the covers and lowered her onto it.

She clung to him, cried out when he came down on top of her, his weight, his heat, his leashed power pressing down on her with just the exact measures of domination and consideration to let her feel his hunger, to make her feel cherished.

She wound herself around him, and he groaned, sank deeper onto her, flooded her with his taste and feel.

After the surreal madness of those minutes in the gardens, she'd shied away from visualizing what would really happen between them. She had nothing to draw on in the realm of intimacy but one crushing disappointment. She couldn't predict anything, had even been afraid to. She'd been scared that reality would only suffer in comparison with fantasy.

She should have known. He was magic. Better than anything her meager imagination could conjure. He was her mate. The one she'd believed existed before life had crushed hope out of her. He was the only one. And she wanted him. All of him. Now. *Now.*

He wrenched himself from her arms, making her feel he'd taken her skin with him. "Slow…I said we'll go slow."

"But I don't need slow. I never needed…but I need you…"

"La, ya ghawyeti." He caught her seeking hands, kissed them, crossed them over her heart. "No, my temptress. You're over-wrought, and this isn't how I want you to feel during our first time. It has to be glorious, memorable. So we'll take our time. As I said we would. I keep my promises, always." He swept the covers over her, tucked her in. He walked to the windows, drew blackout curtains beneath the drapes, plunging the room into almost pitch-darkness. He came back to her, bent and pressed his lips to her mouth with such tenderness, tears welled in her eyes. "Now sleep, *ya hayati.* And dream of me."

Six

Dreams had never been like this.

Dreams had been drab and nonsensical, forgotten even as they blipped their disjointed patterns over the gray landscape of unconsciousness. The ones momentous enough for her to follow, that left a mark on her memory once oblivion lifted, had been filled with replays of loss, of frustrations that would forever echo unresolved.

Now her dreams were vibrant and full of splashes of emotion and gusts of excitement. Blinding in clarity, transporting in delight, open fields of possibility and impossibility, where she flew, soared, right alongside her knight of the desert.

Now they were taking a new turn, for the tangible.

Pleasure rained all over her from warm, gentle caresses, spiced with the scent of maleness, accentuated by the rumbles of cosseting. She filled her arms with the dream, held on. It expanded, pulled back on a lazy purr. "It's incredible to have you devour me in your sleep, *ya gummari,* but I'd rather have you do it awake."

Panicking, she reached out to catch it, and in her alarm, opened her eyes. And something far better than any dream filled her vision, blocked out the world. Shehab.

She moaned his name. The most wonderful thing she'd ever heard or had on her lips. "Shehab..."

The smile he gave her, the indulgence he poured over her made her feel as if she'd melt into the bed beneath her.

He tickled her nose with a lock of her hair. "Are you awake this time, or are we having another sleep-talking session?"

"I love it when you tease...*oh.*" She stormed up to her feet, jumped over him and onto the floor. He too shot to his feet, alarm starting to form on his lips. She squealed, *"Bathroom."*

He laughingly if urgently pointed at a door at the far end of the expansive room. She hurtled there.

After dealing with the emergency, she was thankful for the chance to freshen up. She'd never woken up with another person, wasn't having any interaction with him—the epitome of mouth-watering freshness—before she was squeaky clean.

She was so acutely aware of his presence outside she barely took in the opulence of the all-marble-and-gold-fixtures bathroom as she tried to fix her appearance. Her self-consciousness at being all sleep-swollen and wrinkled increased when she came out to find him, a being out of oriental fables in an outfit made for the desert and sharing its hues and textures, propped up in her bed with his endless legs crossed at the ankles. The one thing that reassured her was that he was looking at her as if she was a hot gourmet meal and he was starving.

She approached him, feeling intensely gauche, her heart stumbling over a thousand insecurities. And incredulity.

God, she was really here. Halfway across the world. On his island. And he was waiting for her to join him in bed, an inexorable magnet when she was a helpless pin. Could this really be happening? She, Farah Beaumont, the ultimate misfit, understood and appreciated, hungered for by this man she hadn't dared to dream existed?

She faltered, looked around dazedly. He'd opened the blackout curtains and light was seeping through the drapes, giving the room that dreamscape quality. How many hours had she slept? Not many, since sunset was around 7:00 p.m., and she'd gone to sleep as soon as he'd left the room, around 1:00 p.m....

One of his hands patted the space beside him, ending her confusion. She jumped there, curled into him like a cat.

"Now that was an emergency," he drawled, amusement staining his magnificent baritone.

Just what she'd thought. She chuckled. "Yeah, which is weird, come to think of it. Say..." She sat up. "Don't you have to go to work, take care of the crisis?"

"I did, for today. I flew out this morning, was in meetings and negotiations for six hours."

"What do you mean six hours? How can you—this morning...?" Then it dawned on her. "God, how long *have* I slept?"

"Do you want the interval in hours, or in days?"

"Days!" She flopped back in his arms. "No wonder there was an emergency." She sat back up, poking him. "Now stop making fun of me *with* me and tell me exactly how long I slept."

Making a visible effort to keep a straight face, he examined his watch. "Considering you've been awake for exactly fifteen minutes and thirty-two seconds now, you slept exactly twenty-six hours, three minutes and...forty-three...*four* seconds."

She poked him, kissed him, groaned against his lips, all at once. "It's all your fault. I never sleep more than six hours."

He surrendered to her, his hands restless on her back, his groans rising as her lips landed anywhere on his face. "I plead guilty. I whisked you away from your world, kept you up for over a day. I should have insisted you got some sleep."

She drew back, ran her hands over his robe-clad shoulders. "There was no way I could sleep while you were awake. But you weren't knocked for a loop staying up so long like I was. You even put in a full day's work with flights *and* fights involved."

He smoothed his hand down her hair. "I sleep little by nature. But with you around, insomnia will enter a new dimension." His eyes fixed on her lips, pulling them by sheer will toward his. Just half a breath away, he whispered, "How about a ride?"

She pulled away, her eyes rounding, a hundred images crashing into her mind. Sculpted flesh, moist with exertion, hard with arousal, beneath her, around her, hands spanning her waist, moving her up, down… "Huh?"

He'd seen everything that had played in her mind, just as clearly as if it had played on a widescreen. She was certain. In response, his lips crooked at one corner, the roughening of his voice the only indication that reading her thoughts had affected him. "*Do* you ride? Horses?"

Oh. *Oh.* "Uh…umm…" She croaked. "Not since I got my scar. It was the last straw. Mom had a fit and insisted that Dad never take me to the ranch again."

"The last straw, eh? So you'd given them one too many scares. But not to worry. I'll give you my most accommodating mare to ride." He dropped a kiss on her nose. "But first, something to eat. You must be starving."

And she was. For him. But he wasn't, for her? She'd thought he'd postponed making love to her because she'd been exhausted. But she was overcharged now. So why wasn't he…?

He pulled her to him, buried his face in her neck, bringing her between his legs, leaving her in no doubt of the extent of his hunger, amazing her once more with his restraint. He groaned when she ground her core into his hardness, unconsciously trying to assuage the ache pounding there. His answering thrust felt as involuntary, riding what sounded like a pained rumble, before his hand on her buttocks ground her harder into him, stopping her from moving and maddening them both further.

His voice was tight with control when he murmured, "We'll spend what remains of the day roaming the island. What we don't cover today, we will in the days to come." His voice dropped an octave. "We have all the time in the world."

He'd read her mind again. And this was his answer. Showing her that he was starving for her, too, with the incontestable evidence of his body. But his words were equally clear.

When he'd said they'd go slow, he'd really meant it.

And suddenly it scared her.

She'd thrown away her wariness at Shehab's first touch, would have braved any recriminations or repercussions to be one with him, once, in those gardens. When he'd offered slower, more, she'd snatched at the offer that was so much better than what she would have happily settled for.

Even when he'd invited her here, she'd had no expectations beyond the satisfaction of her unstoppable desire for him. She'd been ecstatic that someone like him existed, that she provoked the same desire in him, delirious at anticipating what she'd given up on ever experiencing, a man who set her every cell singing with life. She hadn't hoped for a second the affair would last for longer than it took for him to move on. She'd accepted it without the least resentment or longing for more. It would have been enough to last her a lifetime.

But now he was offering her what she'd never dreamed any man would—time. And not just time spent seducing her, but time to savor her, *her,* not her body. As he'd promised, as she hadn't understood, or believed. As she now did.

And she knew what that time would do.

Time would destroy the simplicity of the equation. She wouldn't be satisfied with the purity of a physical and transient relationship. If she got to know the man inside the male, undiluted by physical involvement, she might start to think there could be even more. This was a hurt she wouldn't come back from.

She wanted to beg him not to compound the addiction she could already feel taking hold within her, not to set her up for frustration. For devastation. But for once, something stopped her from confessing her thoughts, her vulnerability. She had no right to burden him with her fears and frailties, to demand that he modify his behavior to observe them. But she could modify her own behavior. If she were sane, she'd lay down her rules and leave if he refused them. But she'd lost her mind…

She should still try to change his.

She slid up his body, rubbing against his unyielding steel, tasting his neck, biting into the sculpture of his lower lip, groaned her plea when he opened to her on a growl of pleasure. "We can explore tomorrow. Today, I only want to explore you…"

He stemmed her entreaty, thrusting into her recesses, draining her until she sagged in his arms. "And you *will* explore me. And I will explore you, claim you, do everything to you."

He surged up, sweeping her around and beneath him and her eyes stung, filled, with relief. And disappointment. There'd be no more waiting. There'd be no more.

But he rose from the bed, in one impossible movement scooping her up in his arms and striding to the other end of the room, entered a huge, exquisitely outfitted dressing room.

He laid her down on a sofa facing a wall-to-wall mirror before heading to the closets paneling the walls. Through a sliding door he gathered clothes that looked like replicas of his, and came back to her. Then he kneeled in front of her. He held one foot after the other, slipped off her sandals, then, as in the gardens, he pressed one to his heart. This time when his lips hovered over her flesh, they descended, made contact.

She arched on a spasm of emotion, at the sight of him, the feel, the very idea of him kissing her foot.

"I've never waited for the gratification of my desires, *ya galbi*." His voice was gruff, driven as he dragged his lips and tongue over the arches of her feet, the backs of her calves, the insides of her thighs. She was quaking, begging when he withdrew, swept the clothes over her lap. "But I can wait if it's for you. I can wait until everything is perfect."

Just perfect.

Farah glowered at the Byzantine-style woodcarving that hung at the entrance to Shehab's stables. The thermometer nestling in its intricacy stood at 112°F. In the shade. She wondered if it was reading the atmosphere's temperature or hers.

Even an hour after that episode in her bedroom, after a perfect meal and a real shower and a change into the clothes he'd picked out for her, she was still sizzling. Everything he did or said kept her simmering. Before leaving her to go and deal with some details, he'd urged her to go inside the stables out of the heat and given her a kiss that had her a breath away from meltdown.

She stumbled into the interior, seeking its coolness. The sun was merciless even during its descent, but Shehab had made sure she was protected from all its dangers. Cool, flowing clothes, constant hydration and her every exposed part covered in sunblock. He'd seen to that himself, with meticulousness that had left her feeling more burned than any ultraviolet exposure could have caused. She'd assured him from distant memory that she'd always handled sun and heat well. He'd countered, not sun like this. She hadn't been built for it, hadn't been drenched in it from birth like he had been. He had to acclimatize her to it gradually, would never forgo any precaution. He couldn't be too careful with her.

She thought he could be. He was. Too careful with her. And it was starting to mess with her sanity.

She pushed her sunglasses over her head. As her vision adjusted, a silver mare materialized out of the gloom, patiently standing in the aisle wearing a saddle and bridle. She was looking straight at her, and, Farah could swear, was stunned to see her. In the next second she whinnied and tossed her head. And, wow, what a beauty.

She'd seen enough *Useel,* purebred Arabian mares, in her father's stables to recognize one. This one was remarkable even by his fanatical standards. Which figured. There was no way Shehab had anything but the best. The horse stood at least 15 hands, with an impressive depth of chest. Her short head had a beautiful concave profile, a broad forehead and wide jowls.

Farah's admiring scrutiny faltered. The mare was trotting toward her, ears tucked, nostrils flared, snorting an unmistakable threat…

"Ablah."

At Shehab's admonition, the mare at once stopped and perked up her ears, her prominent eyes all but grinning sheepishly.

Farah swung around to him. "I hope *that's* not your most accommodating mare."

"Actually, she is." He caught his lower lip in his teeth, his face ablaze with wickedness. "I like my horses spirited."

"Yeah, and it seems you train them as guard dogs, too."

"She doesn't usually see strangers. She was probably wary of you."

She smirked. "She didn't seem wary to me, and I'm no longer sure I want to reprise my long-bygone equine experience."

He gave her a considering look, then turned to the mare.

"Ablah…*ta'ee hena.*" Ablah trotted to him at once, nuzzled him in the shoulder. He held her face in his hands, murmured in Arabic. Ablah shifted uncomfortably, looking positively shamefaced.

Farah was incredulous. "What did you say to her?"

He gave Ablah a stern look. "That I was upset with her because she wasn't nice to you, that you're the woman I crave."

"That's supposed to make her more amenable toward me? I bet that's why she wasn't nice. She's jealous as hell."

He huffed a chuckle. "She's a horse, Farah."

"She's a *mare,* Shehab. I bet you have females of every species swooning within a hundred-mile radius."

He flashed her a smile that left her wanting to flip down her sunglasses. "Though I'd be appalled to think every female rat and shrimp around were wiggling their whiskers at me, I'll snap this up as the compliment I'm sure you meant." She narrowed her eyes at him, stuck out her tongue. He laughed, pinched her cheek softly. "I can assure you Ablah won't try to get rid of the competition. But if you're not comfortable, I'll ride her, and you can ride Barq." He patted the neck of the other horse, which a stable hand had just led up to them, placing the reins in Shehab's hand. "*He's* taken with *you.*"

Farah looked at Barq, a magnificent black stallion who looked decidedly more docile than Ablah and who was checking her out with interest. She looked back into the mare's eyes, almost saw the impish challenge there, then she shook her head. "Nah, I think I'll get acquainted with Ablah. I'm sure we can come to an understanding, one lady to another."

His smile brightened with approval. "That's *jameelati,* always doing the unexpected."

"Yeah, let's just hope I don't really do the unexpected and spend my sabbatical in traction. Say, what does *Ablah* mean?"

"'Perfectly formed.' *Barq* means 'lightning.'"

Farah eyed the magnificent mare, then sighed. "And she knows it, too. And if Barq's name is also descriptive, I'd say it's a good choice I opted to ride Ablah."

He gathered her to him, tilted up her face to his. "You do know I wouldn't propose riding either if I wasn't certain you'd be totally safe?" She nodded, smiled her total trust up at him. His smile widened as he half kneeled beside her offering a leg up. "Up you go."

She put her foot in the stirrup, grabbed the saddle and let him boost her up only for Ablah to give a distressed whinny when she landed on her back.

"Oh, c'mon. So I'm no lightweight, but your master out-weighs me by…" she eyed him hungrily, gave her lips an invol-untary lick "…seventy pounds, at least. So quit pretending you're about to keel under my weight."

Ablah snorted, swished her tail. Shehab laughed at the dialogue between woman and mare. Then he bent to Ablah and murmured in her ear, his eyes on Farah. *Et'addebi.*

Ablah fell silent at once, stood motionless and stared ahead, like a soldier, all obedience and steadfastness.

Farah giggled. "What was that? A magic word?"

His eyes glittered pure onyx in the declining sun slanting through the wide-open doors. "Behave."

She wanted to cry out that she was behaving, had already used up her courage in propositioning him, would never make a move again. Then she realized he'd just been translating.

But, no. He was also warning her not to try again to end the time he was bound on having together without sexual intimacy.

Before she could say anything, he swung up on Barq's back and leaned toward her, lowered her sunglasses over her eyes, put his on, pulled Barq's reins, rapped Ablah's rump lightly, and the two horses fell into step with each other.

* * *

Shehab kept within an arm's reach of Farah for the first few hundred feet, murmuring directions and encouragements until she was whooping in unbridled joy as she gained confidence, began to rise and fall with the rhythm of Ablah's medium sustained gallop, the wind weaving its hot, dry fingers through her hair, sending it flowing behind her like living bronze fire.

And he again had to acknowledge that it was nothing short of a miracle. That he was out here, taking her on a tour of the island, instead of back in her bed, taking her, period. That he'd taken her riding, instead of having her ride him.

And she'd wanted to, had entreated him to let her.

The only way he'd accessed the unsuspected power that had enabled him to say no was that this torture had a flipside. In prolonging her seduction, he found himself reveling in the bittersweet anticipation, the burgeoning arousal.

Exhilaration bubbled inside him in answer to her unfettered enjoyment. He shouted to her over the whipping of wind and the staccato of hooves, "You're a natural horsewoman, *ya saherati.*"

"It's Ablah who's a natural rookie mare," she shouted back, giggling. "You were right. She is riding herself, so to speak, keeping me miraculously glued to her back."

From then on they kept exchanging smiles and shouted comments, laughing at anything the other said.

He gave her a thorough guided tour, and she was the perfect tourist, gratifyingly interested and impressed. Then at the highest point on the island where both its sides could be seen, he brought them to a stop, carried her down from Ablah and to the spread beneath the shade tent he'd had erected for them.

He sat down, took her across him, one knee supporting her back, her breasts pressing against his chest, her buttocks against his erection. He took the lips she offered, thrust into the sweet-

ness she surrendered, drew back only when torment lost the
sweet edge, the bitter side beginning to cut deep, looked down
into the emerald eyes that truly rivaled the crystalline shores of
his island. So willing, so giving, so trusting…

No. Willing, yes. Giving, no. She wanted only to take. He
must never lose sight of that.

Snatching his eyes away from her spell, he continued her
education. "On that side of the island, the water is knee-high for
over two miles before deepening very gradually. On the other,
the depth drops hundreds of feet at once." He cocked his head at
her. "Do you swim?"

"I haven't swum in over ten years, but I was quite the fish
when Dad was alive…" She stopped, bit her lip.

Every time she mentioned the man she'd lived her life believing was her real father, her mood plunged. He wanted to probe,
was burning to hear her version of why she'd so vehemently
rejected the new father fate had sent her.

But no. At the merest slipup, she'd sensed she was being manipulated. He couldn't afford another mistake.

He gathered her closer, cupped her breast. "So you're a
mermaid for real. I knew it." He succeeded in distracting her as
she melted in his hold, thrust her firmness in his hand for him to
do what he would with it. He groaned as the dual-bladed weapon
he used on her cut deeper into him. "It's another perfection, *ya
aroosat bahri*—my mermaid. By daylight, I'll take you to the
deep end, plunge you into the dimension of the coral reefs, and
by moonlight, we'll roam the shallows, soak in them."

She shuddered at the images he evoked, and he moved to the
next step in her sensory overload. He cleaned his hands, produced
refreshments from the hamper he'd arranged, poured her some,
put the tiny crystal hourglass-shaped glass to her lips.

She took a sip, moaned appreciatively, "Mmm—what's that?"

"The famed Arabian coffee…a brew of lightly roasted special beans and cardamom. For best effect you eat this with it…"

She unquestioningly opened for the dried date he put to her lips, moaned as she described the incredible chewiness, the caramelized flavor. After he had her finish three cups and half a packet, he began fondling her lips, prodding her to lick his fingers clean of the stickiness. She was soon sucking him in earnest, every pull lodging in his erection, where he almost felt those lips performing the same abandoned ritual. He pulled his fingers out of her mouth, clamped her between his knees, stilling her movements before he exploded. "I said behave."

The eyes that had gone smoky jade with arousal turned a disconcerted bottle-green at his growl.

It made him rush to add, "If you do, I'll take you to see the burst of flowers and grass that followed the outpouring of rain a couple of weeks ago, before the green carpet dries and dies under the blistering sun. We might catch some of the island's inhabitants taking a snack, wild rabbits, gazelles…"

She lurched in his arms, her forlorn expression burning away in a blast of delight. "Gazelles? You have gazelles here?"

He nodded. "A population of over 300 roaming freely."

She whooped, spilled from his arms, jumped to her feet, pulled at him. "Get up, get up. Let's go see them." Her face fell again as soon as he stood up. "Oh, man, I don't have a camera, not even my phone." Her brightness dimmed completely as she exhaled. "They'll probably run away when we approach, anyway."

He produced his phone for her. "Capture everything to your heart's content. And, no, they won't run. They're used to me and the horses. You can even feed them, if you like."

"*If* I like?" she squeaked. "If a gazelle eats from my hand, I'll just die, and die happy!"

"Adjust that to live and live happy, and I'll make certain you feed gazelles, *ya gummari,* today, in their natural habitat. Then I'll bring a few to the mansion for you to feed regularly."

She bounced up and down before smothering him in exuberant hugs. "Thank you, thank you...for giving me this." She withdrew, threw her arms open wide. "And all of this."

He stared at her. Could this woman who was in ecstasies at the idea of hand-feeding gazelles be real? How could she coexist with the one who'd manipulated her aging lover into agreeing to her leaving on her latest fling, into even apologizing for being upset about it and begging for an assurance that she'd miss him? An assurance she'd given as she'd devoured *him* with her eyes?

His smile felt like it was digging into his flesh as he struggled to keep it pinned on. "I've done nothing yet, *ya galbi.* I want to give you the whole world."

Her eyes became mossy-green. "Oh, Shehab, it's wonderful of you to say that. But what would I do with the whole world? I'd take gazelles to pet and feed over that any day." With that she whooped again, swung away, ran back to Ablah.

He was determined not to rush to her. Never giving her what she wanted when she wanted it was the only way to stop her from winning the battle she didn't know they were having.

Then she turned to him, a fantasy out of his land's richest fables, shimmering in the flowing robes of its deserts, incandescent in her excitement, overpowering in her eagerness.

And he gave in, obeyed. He rushed to her.

"...with slow, graceful wing movements, the black-backed manta ray flew through the water like a giant alien bird."

Shehab's words caressed her nape as he helped her put on her wetsuit. She sighed, let it all wash over her. His heat and presence, his yacht's gentle undulations, the early morning sun's warmth, the salty breeze's purity. It all coalesced into this incredible new world he'd let her enter, let her share in its adventures. He kept telling her of the many that she hadn't been there to share before the last glorious two weeks—weeks that had washed away a lifetime of city dwelling and aloneness, had taken over her memory. She could barely remember her life before them.

Hypnotized, she hung on every syllable of his latest tale.

"It was over twenty-five feet across and I could have swum into its mouth as it gaped to sieve plankton-laden water." He turned her, smoothing her suit, raising her zipper and her longings. "Then it stopped in front of me. Its huge eyes gazed at me for a moment, then with an elegant flip of its wings, it banked away. I was nine and it was my first plunge into the coral reef. Meeting that gentle monster gave me a taste of the underwater world I knew would take me a lifetime to explore. I never wanted to leave, but it took me almost two decades to realize my boyhood dream, when I finally owned this place."

She exhaled, almost in tears at imagining him as a boy falling under the spell of this island's diverse magic. "And it's magnificent. I feel privileged you wanted to share it with me."

And she felt more than privileged. She felt blessed.

Two weeks ago she'd been scared that emotions would consume her. But this was too glorious. She'd live it at any cost, wouldn't wish for more. For what more could there be? This was everything. The man of beyond her dreams, patiently lavishing his care on her, even as hunger escalated. The last time he'd drawn back from the precipice, she'd wept, and his distress had been as deep.

But soon, he wouldn't draw back, and she'd be his. She already was. She'd be his forever. It didn't matter how long he remained in her life, the life she'd thought she'd live inert, undiscovered. He'd recognized her, unearthed everything that had lain dormant and useless inside her and brought it to life.

She loved him. Would always love him. And her love would always be the best part of her life, the one to give it meaning.

And when his path swerved from hers forever, she'd be happy she'd had that much. The lifetime's worth of wonders he'd shown her, in the reef, in the air, on land. But the true wonders had been what he'd shown her of him, the companion, the playmate, the incomparable man. She couldn't wait for the next wonder.

She ran her hand over his sculpted torso in the confines of his own wetsuit. "What will you show me today?" He'd been teaching her to dive since the second day they'd been there.

"Today we dive a little deeper. If you think you're ready."

"Oh, I'm ready."

And she was. Ready for anything at all with him.

After he helped her with her diving gear, double-checked everything, they dove into the luminous green waters. He'd told her it was now infinitely more beautiful to him for echoing her eyes. Their descent was like slow-motion skydiving, a sublime philosophical experience, a plunge into an alien world.

Once they were hovering in a blue-green nothing where she could see neither surface nor bottom, she saw something huge moving in the distance. She clutched his arm in alarm. He soothed her, gestured for her to watch as the shape began to resemble a compact swarm of bees. It turned out to be a school of striated, anchovylike fish. He tugged at her, and they flowed smoothly toward it only for a tunnel to open up in the wall of fish, engulfing them. Her heart thundered with excitement as he hugged her and they swam in what felt like a cave with moving walls as the uncountable fish moved as one all around them as if guided by a single brain, turning the fusion of their own limbs into a dance of oneness she'd never imagined could exist.

He guided them out and gestured for her to watch. He suddenly kicked toward the fish and the school packed itself into a giant ball. The moment he touched it, the ball exploded.

Exhilarated at the fish fireworks he'd treated her to, she clapped as he swam back to her. He made a theatrical gesture, accepting her adulation before clamping her to his side and propelling her up slowly, his light revealing an explosion of color from the fan coral that grew out from the reef wall, their stunning, feathery tentacles constantly performing a rhythmic dance, opening and closing in unison like beckoning hands.

Their legs tangled in their short wetsuits, rubbing in the silk of the fluid dream they were enveloped in. And she couldn't bear it anymore. She'd beg him for an end of the waiting today.

Suddenly she saw a striated red, yellow and black lionfish hovering behind him, incredibly beautiful fins flowing, long spines separated and—and...*poisonous.*

The certainty of this once-learned knowledge flooded her with panic as the fish approached Shehab's back, bending its own like a snake. She pounced on him, swept around him, exchanging places. The next second pain shot between her shoulder blades, as if she'd been skewered by a red-hot poker.

Her scream gurgled into her regulator.

Seven

Farah would remember what happened after the lionfish stung her in the same way she did her garbled dreams.

She'd felt as if she were outside her pain-ridden body, watching as Shehab swept her up in his arms and torpedoed to the surface before hauling her onto the deck of his yacht as if she weighed no more than a few pounds, not her hundred and forty plus the diving gear.

She lay in a state of shock, the white-hot agony lodged in the middle of her back the one thing telling her this wasn't a dream. She watched him as he frantically took off his gear, pounced on hers. The moment he divested her of her goggles and breathing equipment the tears and sobs they'd been stifling seeped out of her burning eyes and lips.

His hands were shaking with urgency as he stripped her down to her swimsuit, turned her to her side to examine her injury. At the sight, he inhaled a sharp, taxed breath, reached for something that looked like a walkie-talkie and ground out a string of Arabic, his eyes feverish on her.

Then he threw the thing aside, scooped her up and rushed to the shade of the upper sitting area, placing her on a couch on her side so it wouldn't chafe against her injury before tearing open a first-aid kit and rummaging through it for a tube, his movements slowing down and gentling only after he produced gel from it and carefully applied it to the sting. She moaned as a freezing sensation poured over the burning, her flaccid body going rigid against the bombardment of confusing signals. He soothed her with hands and voice. The spasm passed, and she felt the whole area going numb. She blinked at his blurred image only to wince at his fierceness and focus, barely managed a rasped, "Thanks."

"Thanks? *Ya Ullah*, why did you *do* that?" She stared at him. Was he mad at her? Or was she hallucinating as the poison coursed through her system? Would she die now? "I told you never to approach anything you don't know, to look but never touch. But you almost attacked that lionfish and it struck back so hard its spine penetrated your wetsuit. And it could have been worse, a stonefish…" He stopped, his face working, his fists bunching.

From a long distance she heard herself stuttering, "I'm s-sorry…b-but a-all I knew was it's poisonous and it was going to sting you…"

He went totally still. His face drained of all agitation and expression. Froze. And her ears were filling with thunder.

Then she was again watching it all happen to someone else as Shehab swooped down on her, carried her to the deck where she realized the thunder wasn't blood roaring in her ears, but his helicopter, which, it turned out, could land on water. He had her inside, she didn't register how, in the back, secured on a stretcher, then stood up to strip down to his knee-length swimming trunks before kneeling beside her.

She lost all perception of time as the flight ended and he rushed with her in his arms into the mansion, his men streaking before them, opening doors. But this time he took a different path, one leading somewhere she'd never been before.

The sensation of wading in a dream thickened as he swept her through what felt like endless spaces shrouded in dimness and incense, their Spartan sparseness stamped by virility and power. This must be his quarters. Her gaze clung to the huge bed, a bed she'd longed to share with him. Now she might never share it…

Consciousness surged as lights rose, illuminating the space he'd crossed into. The impression of moving through the landscape of *One Thousand and One Nights* intensified as she gaped around the gigantic, all-marble-and-stone chamber. It interconnected on each side with two others, each space ringed with arches supported by tapering columns. The middle chamber, which he'd just entered, sprawled beneath a soaring dome dotted by circular bottle-glass openings that let sunbeams slash through the half light permeating the place, pouring from the semi-opened windows that ringed the walls beneath the dome.

He gave her no chance to linger over details as he rushed to the chamber on the right. It was dominated by a shallow rectangular pool, tiled in checkered black-and-beige marble. He lowered her onto a long stone seat with utmost care before rushing away. He calibrated some mechanism at the wall, hurried back, jogged her out of her stupor by scooping her up again. She opened groggy eyes to find him stepping into the pool. Her thoughts swirled in confusion, wondering why he considered giving her a bath important as he lowered them both into the water. And she screamed. *It was boiling.*

He restrained her, his arms cleaving her back to his chest, his legs imprisoning hers. "Shh…shh…*ya galbi,* it must be done."

"You must…boil me?" She twisted in his arms, unable to bear the scalding heat. "And…you're boiling…yourself, too…"

He only lay back in the water, submerging them both, then clamped his limbs around her tighter and crooned, "The water temperature is only 114°F."

"Only?" she whimpered, the initial shock passing, only for the full measure of discomfort to register, every cell overheating, every drop of moisture pushing to the surface, flooding out, getting lost in the surrounding water.

He kept her submerged, his hands and voice gentleness itself. "I know it's very uncomfortable, but it's for the sting."

She thrashed her head against his chest, feeling as if she were suffocating one cell at a time, her lifeforce seeping out of her every pore. "But I don't feel it anymore."

"That's the effect of the local anesthetic, but it isn't a treatment for the poison. Only high heat can stop it."

"So—I won't die?" she choked, just now realizing she'd been too numb to think, to be really scared.

"*Ya Ullah,* you thought the poison was fatal?" She nodded, shook her head, nodded again. He let out a dark groan as he hugged her tighter, burying his face in her neck. "The one with fatal consequences is the stonefish's sting. The worst of the lionfish's is the pain, which is excruciating. I tried to catch one when I was eleven. Yes, we were both reckless at that age. So I have first-hand experience with the agony you suffered. But the poison isn't to be treated lightly. If not neutralized by heat, it would have coursed through your blood until you started vomiting before you lost consciousness from hypotension."

"I was starting to get queasy…thought it was a sign of—of…"

He turned her face to his, stemmed the rest of her projection in his mouth, his growl reverberating inside her.

Her consciousness was slipping away when he wrenched his lips from hers and heaved them both out of the water. "Enough. Any more heat and you'll faint from heatstroke."

She shuddered hard as the cooler air hit her. He tightened his hold around her as he stepped out of the pool and strode to the middle chamber. She lay limply in his arms, her head cushioned by his muscles, her bleary eyes taking in a raised marble platform of purest white right below the center of the fenestrated dome. It seemed to glow in the unearthly illumination. Or maybe her vision was all fuzzy. Whatever it was, it felt like a continuation of her journey into the dream.

Images invaded her mind, her nerve endings, of Shehab, naked, lying face down on the marble as steam swirled around his magnificent body, his muscles glistening, their tautness after a grueling day's negotiations relaxing under her hands, all hers to caress and cosset, to tease and taste.

He put her on the platform as if he were placing a priceless work of art on a pedestal, and her imagination made a sharp turn to him rising from his surrender to her pampering, yanking her to his slick, hot flesh, letting her feel what she'd done to him before laying her down on the marble…

The sequence shattered as her sweltering skin touched the cool marble for real. He leaned over her, one arm at the back of her thighs, the other at her upper back, his face flushed to copper, drenched in sweat, clenched in anxiety as he seemed to count her breaths. "How are you feeling now, *ya galbi?*"

She gulped around the thick, dry thing that used to be her tongue. "Thirsty."

He let out some expletive in Arabic, some self-abuse by the look on his face, laid her down completely before streaking away. She turned a head that felt filled with seawater, saw him disappear into his bedroom. He seemed to reappear at once, carrying two bottles and two glasses. He filled each glass from a bottle, scooped her up, put the first glass to her lips and his lips to her temple. "Drink, *ya galbi.*"

She did, and with every gulp of cool water felt every cell surging with clarity and energy once more.

After the second glass of water, he gave her the other drink. She sampled it, winced at the sourness of the first sip, before she fully tasted its richness, the complexity of flavors. She drank it all down thirstily, moaning her enjoyment.

As she began the second glassful she asked, "What's this?"

"It's a special cocktail of mine, one I use after extreme workouts, a mixture of hibiscus, carob, sugar cane, pomegranate and a few desert fruits, mostly *daum* and *hab'bel azeez.*"

"It's amazing. An elixir." She finished the second glass. "Feels like all the vital stuff I lost from sweating gallons is back in residence. In other news, I can feel my back again, so the anesthetic must have worn off. But since I feel no pain and I guess this is me thinking straight again, it seems your trying to make soup out of me worked." He winced, still anxious as his eyes roamed over her. She leaned back in his embrace, her hand following the slash of his cheekbone lovingly. "I'm fine now. You saved me."

He turned his lips into her palm, planted a hot, shuddering kiss. "Only because you saved me."

"But I didn't. It turned out there was no real danger."

"There was. It might not be fatal, but the pain can be inca-pacitating, and the poison is disorienting. And then you didn't know that was the extent of the danger when you took the sting. *Ya Ullah*—that you did that, endangered yourself for me…"

Something painful thrummed inside her chest at the agonized look in his eyes. She didn't want him to feel bad about it. She never wanted him to feel bad about anything for a second.

She caught his face in her hands. "You would have done the same for me. And it was better me than you. There was no way I could have gotten you out of the water. Seems through my mess of half-learned knowledge and panic, I made a decision that turned out to be rational, volunteering as the victim of choice."

His grated his teeth. "And you're never going to do something like that again. Swear it to me now. You'll never put yourself at risk. Not for anyone or anything."

His intensity shook her. She'd already acknowledged the inescapability of loving him, but she had to cling to a bit of herself, unsurrendered to him. Otherwise she wouldn't know how to exist when it was over.

Escaping both his fervor and her thoughts, she pretended lightness. "I never swear. Dad drilled that into me." At his aggrieved glance at her deliberate misinterpretation, she rushed on, "And then, all's well that ends well, OK? I may have ruined our dive, but think of it this way. I managed to arm you with one more adventure on this island. Now how about we concentrate on important stuff? Like the fact that you have your own honest-to-goodness Turkish bath? This is the steam room, right?"

His eyebrows dipped at her obvious sidetracking maneuver. "The *hararet,* yes. A Turkish word that comes from the Arabic *hararah,* or heat. You're distracting me, right?"

Her smile was tremulous and entreating. "Is it working?"

His hold tightened from solicitous to possessive, his gaze melting from aggravated to devouring. "You need only to breathe, to exist, to distract me, to be the one thing I can think of. Don't you know that by now?"

Suddenly her body filled with a spike of longing beyond her endurance. "All I know is, when I was disoriented, I could only think that even though every moment we've had together has been the best thing that has ever happened to me, I still felt incomplete because you didn't…because we didn't…and that it was now too late."

* * *

Farah's words ripped through Shehab like shrapnel, tore away the barrier he'd erected to suspend thought until she was safe.

And the enormity of what she'd done sank through him.

She'd put herself between him and mortal danger.

He'd never thought such a sacrifice possible from someone other than his brothers, Farooq and Kamal, or bodyguards who made their livelihoods selling their bodies as shields. He'd never even expected that any of the people who populated his life, in permanence or transit, would sacrifice a measure of their well-being for him. And for Farah to offer the ultimate sacrifice, her very life for his, was beyond comprehension. Beyond endurance.

He'd brought her here to seduce her. He'd struggled each moment to remind himself she was a means to an end. He'd fought to convince himself that no matter how much he craved her, and though he *would* marry her, there'd never be emotions involved.

But with each moment he could no longer connect the reality of the woman who delighted him, who roused every appreciative emotion he'd never thought he had, with the image of the unfeeling, amoral woman she was supposed to be. Then came today.

Memories bombarded him now that she was no longer in pain or danger. Of every heart-bursting second as she'd charged him, exchanging places with him. As he'd watched her convulse, felt her scream gurgle through the water, electrocuting him with fright. And then what followed, where only the blinding need to carry her to safety, to absorb her fear and agony, had existed.

And here she was, dismissing her action, refusing credit, making light of it. Then worse, painting him a nightmarish alternate reality when she could have slipped through his fingers never to be reached again. Then came the worst of all. Showing him that her only regret, in the moments when she'd thought she might die, was that she'd die without experiencing intimacy with him.

Before today, he'd started to think maybe he didn't have to seduce her all the way, could finalize their marriage then leave it up to her whether they consummated it. He'd thought that might make his deception sting less when she found out about it, give them a chance to work out a viable relationship.

But she'd made him face the horror of the possibility of loss at any moment, and in their situation, of the extra desolation of losing without ever having lived the pleasure.

He could swear he heard the last of his control buckling.

Blind, out of his mind, he caught her to him, filled his hands with her, honey and life and unconditional surrender made flesh, made woman, all woman. And she was his for the taking. And he would take her. And take her.

"Ana ella ensan," he groaned over and over in the sweetness she surrendered with such mind-destroying eagerness, to himself, to the fates that had placed her, a temptation he couldn't resist, a test he was bound to fail, in his path. "Just human…"

He tore his lips away, sank down to her ample cleavage. She clamped his head to her flesh, stopping his movements, gasped, "If you're going to stop…please, stop now."

He shook off her feeble restraint gently, dragged his teeth along her honeyed swell, looked from that incredible vantage into her eyes, saw the distress bordering on hurt. It was real.

Everything about her was real.

And he groaned all that was real inside him, too. "I only stopped before, at the price of pieces of my sanity, because I feared that intimacy, if indulged too fast, would overwhelm us, that other pleasures would go undiscovered under its blinding effect. But I can't bear that you felt such loss because of the restraint I imposed, thinking I was building up anticipation…"

She struggled up on one elbow, her other arm hooking around his neck, her face blazing with anxiety. "And it was glorious, Shehab, *glorious*. You gave me so much, on so many levels, every bit unprecedented and irreplaceable. Experiences I never thought to have. I just got greedy, thinking how much more it would be if…"

He took her hand off his neck, pushed her back gently until he had her flat on her back on the platform, loomed above her, his gaze greedy on her face and breasts, which shuddered with emotion. "And you were absolutely right. It will be beyond what either of us has ever dreamed possible. I'll worship you, brand you, turn your body into an instrument of ecstasy, yours and mine. You're mine to pleasure as I will, aren't you?"

Her nod was frantic. "Yes, I'm yours…yours, Shehab."

Yours. His. *Mine.* The concept seared through him, becoming mind-bending fact as he looked down on her, peach-flushed through the perfection of her tan, her pupils engulfing the emerald, crimson lips swollen with his passion, panting for more, beckoning him to come lose his mind, once and for all.

"Yes, Farah, you're mine, and I'll do everything to you, for you, with you…" He dragged down the straps of her swimsuit, exposing her an inch at a time to the rhythm of his words, drawing a whimper at each glide, replacing its cover with his lips, tongue and teeth, coating her velvet firmness in suckles and nibbles, knowing just where to skim and tantalize, where to linger and torment, where to draw harder and devour. Her moans became cries, then keens, then labored gasps.

The pressure in his loins, the accumulation of need was reaching critical levels. He feared it would be like a dam breaking the moment he thrust inside her. And he couldn't let their first intimacy be anything less than perfect bliss. And it was no longer because he needed her in his total power. Now the only reality was that he craved her pleasure far more than he craved his, that his pleasure would stem from hers.

He took pity on her, on himself, slid the swimsuit all the way off her, lingering on a long groan as he slid one foot out after the other. Then he stood back, his heart thundering, looking down on her, laid out before him like an unending feast.

He'd seen almost all of her before, her breasts on their first night, the rest of her in one-piece swimsuits that left little to the imagination. Or so he'd thought. For there she was. Beyond his imagination. Ripe, strong, tailored to his every fastidious taste and beyond. His female. And she was dying for him as he was for her, quaking with the force of her need.

"Enti ar'oa memma kont atasawar…" He heard the awe in his voice, knew it was real. Everything he felt was real. More real than anything he'd ever felt before. "More incredible than I've imagined. And *ya Ullah, ya* Farah, how I've imagined…"

She held her arms out in demand, in supplication, and he yanked her to him, bending her over one arm, her breasts an erotic offering to sacrifice anything for. Pouring litanies of passion into her lips, all over her face, he kneaded and weighed one breast, seeking one erect, deep-peach nipple, pinching and rolling it before he moved down, captured the other bud of overpowering femininity and need in his mouth.

She screamed. With each pull, she screamed again, shuddered apart. His hands glided over her abdomen, closed over her trim mound, stilled. This. Her core. Where he'd merge them, where he'd invade her, where she'd capture him. And she was letting him have it, own it. He squeezed his eyes, her flesh.

Just as she cried out again, he slid two fingers between the velvet slickness of her exquisite folds, spreading them, getting drunk with the scent of her arousal, the evidence of her desire and dependence made nectar. She was ready for him.

He slipped a careful finger inside her, needing to know how much, and grunted with another blast of arousal. Soaking, for him, but…so tight. And she lurched, as if he'd hurt her.

So not so ready for him. But ready for pleasure. And how he'd pleasure her.

He stroked her, spread honey from her slit before his fingers made way for his thumb to find the knot of flesh where her nerves converged, her trigger. The moment he touched it, he felt as if he'd touched the core of the sun, her cries of pleasure, of his name, strangled, and she bucked in his arms, coming apart in an instantaneous orgasm.

He roared with pride as he drew out her release, rode its waves, easing two fingers inside her clamping flesh, stroking her inside and out until she sobbed into his mouth. He paused inside her depths, loosening her, nipping her nipples until he felt her flesh rippling around his fingers then began to stroke, until tension reinvaded her body and she was thrashing again.

"Shehab please…I n-need you."

For answer, he spread her core, bent, gave her one long lick. She bucked off the platform. "Please, Shehab…you…*you*…"

He subdued her with one hand flat on her abdomen. "I've been starving for you, give me everything you have."

She still tried to squeeze her legs closed, her eyes wet and beseeching. She was shy? How, when she was so experienced?

But nothing he'd been told mattered. His instincts told him she *wasn't*, that his wild flower of the desert had never allowed anyone this privilege. But she would give it to him, and the privilege would be his alone, now and forever.

He invoked his claim. "Aren't you mine?"

She nodded mutely, her color dangerous.

He hooked his forearms below her knees, slid her forward, gliding her over the smoothness slick from her sweat until he had her feet propped against the platform's edge, her thighs spread. He withdrew to look on his arrangement, Farah, open and willing for his ministrations. She overpowered him with her surrender. Blood was a geyser in his head, in his erection. He gritted his teeth, kneeled in front of her, spreading her shaking legs, his hands and lips and teeth devouring their every inch, before he slid her forward until her buttocks were in his hands, bringing her core to him. Her fists bunched, her body tensed up.

"Don't be shy, *ya hayati*. Sit up and watch me worship you, pleasure you, own your every secret. Promise you'll look me in the eye as I bring you to orgasm this time."

She squirmed, hiccupped, then finally nodded, and sat up.

He spread her core, groaned as lust jackknifed in his system. "*Hada ajmal ma ra'ait wa ah'sast*—the most beautiful thing I've ever seen, felt." Overwhelmed, he licked around her lips, capturing them between pulling lips and massaging teeth, circling her trigger, subduing her gently as she bucked with each nip and lick and pull, bringing her to the edge, listening to her explicit pleasure, feeling her flood with it, surge with heat, hurtling toward completion. The moment before it all burst, he blew on her quivering, engorged flesh, withdrew his stimulation until she simmered, keened. He placed a palm on her heart until he felt it start to miss beats. Then he tongue-lashed her trigger and she shredded her throat on ecstasy, unraveled her body on a chain reaction of convulsions. And she looked him in the eyes all through. It was the most erotic, most intimate, most fulfilling experience of his life.

But then, every experience with her had been that.

Now he would take her, and union with her would reinvent the terms of eroticism, intimacy and fulfillment. He prayed she was ready enough now.

First, to bring her to fever pitch again.

He slid up her sweat-slick body, flattening her to the marble, soaking up her drugged look, the looseness confessing the depth of her satisfaction.

But as soon as he branded her lips, letting her taste her pleasure on his, her breath hitched, her hips undulated against him, urgent, insistent. She was aroused that much, that fast again? He hadn't even started stimulating her…

He withdrew to make sure, and she tore at his swimsuit. "I want to see you—all of you…please…"

Hearing the last pillar in his mind give, he snatched at her lips with rough, moist kisses, nothing left in him but the corrosive need to bury himself inside her.

He tore off his swimsuit. She fell to her back, held out her arms, her eyes streaming her plea for him.

He climbed on top of the platform, covered her, felt her softness cushioning his hardness. She opened her legs, and as he'd long dreamed, he guided them over his waist.

Then it registered. Her coolness, her shuddering.

Ya Ullah, how oblivious could he get? After the blows her body had received, her heat-regulating system must be shot.

He withdrew from her and she cried out. *"Shehab…"*

He made her a pacifying gesture, strode below the arches to a wardrobe nestled in the curved marble walls, produced a *pestamal* shawl and hurried back. He covered her, stood back and marveled at how the red, gold and bronze striped cloth seemed to be made to match her blush-tinged tan, her hundred-shades hair.

She tried to cling to him and he bent to her lips. "I'm going nowhere, *ya galbi.* I'll be back in seconds."

Farah watched him coming back in the seconds he'd promised with steam already billowing around him, a colossus of virile beauty stepping from the shroud of myth and time.

She felt parched again as she watched the vapors entwining with the evocative lighting, drenching the whole exotic setup in a mystical, hypnotic ambiance, worshiping the perfect sculpture of his endless shoulders and chest, his cabled arms and ridged abdomen. Then her eyes fell on the wrap around his waist, very much like the one he'd covered her with, parting on one rippling, muscled thigh with every step, tenting on an erection that rattled her with arousal and intimidation.

She lay back, struck mute, her dry mouth suddenly watering, her core cramping, dizzy with the aftershocks of what he'd done to her. Ready for more. For anything. Then he came to stand over her and the sunbeams cascading from the bottle-glass openings in the dome above poured on him, illuminating slashes across his beloved face and glistening, aroused body.

"Let me warm you, *ya galbi.*" His croon was hot, dark molasses pouring over her, making her realize how cold she'd been. But warmth was spreading through her now, generated by the wrap, the steam. And what had flames licking through her nerves was the heat of his hands running up her legs and thighs, kneading, bringing circulation gushing back through her limbs. Then he turned her onto her belly, dragged the wrap to cover her legs, exposing everything above them.

"*T'janenni, ya galbi*...mind-blowing..." he groaned in her ear before he trailed kisses and suckles all over her back. She squirmed with the incredible new sensations, tried to wriggle around, put her stinging hands on him. A hand in the small of her back kept her in place, before it joined with the other to radiate along her back, following what had to be some magical rite's patterns. His hands pressed into muscles, smoothed away aches, sought secrets, found triggers she didn't know she had, comforting, teasing, igniting. He at last spread her buttocks, massaged them, bent to taste and nibble their clenching flesh, concentrating where the scar he hadn't seen before was. In that helpless position, unable to move or see him, with unadulterated sensations lancing from his fingertips and lips and tongue to bombard her womb, her eyes glazed on the scene that filled her vision, something right out of a sultan story.

Then he climbed over her, taking his weight on elbows and knees but still covering her from shoulders to thighs, imprinting her with his power and potency before he bent to suckle at her pulse-point, hard, driving his mark deep, jacking up the level of his torture by arousal. Then he started talking, and life expectancy became a serious issue.

"I'm already addicted to your taste. I want to have you flowing, have you hurtle over one edge after another so I can have my fill. Do you know how you sound at the peak of pleasure? I want you screaming my name like that as you climax around me over and over. I want to feel those velvet muscles that wrung my fingers wringing me of every drop of pleasure."

She was shaking so hard her teeth chattered, and it had nothing to do with being cold. She was coming apart with over-stimulation. "Shehab, I can't breathe…my heart…it's stampeding…don't torment me anymore…please…*take me.*"

Hearing her say the words, *take me,* sobbed on her siren's voice, sabotaged the last of Shehab's reason.

"*Umrek, ya rohi,* command me…" He unclasped their bodies, slid off the platform, turned her, slid her to the edge, brought her trembling thighs around his hips, took hers in one hand, the other bringing his shaft to her entrance, sliding its head into her nectar, spreading it, stimulating her more, lubricating himself, struggling with the need to ram inside her.

When she whimpered again, arched up to seek more of him,

to bring him inside her, he surrendered, flexed his hips, plunged halfway into her heat, going blind with the blast of pleasure.

When his sight returned, he saw her, arched off the platform, the sensations slashing across her face dominated by shock, by pain. The tightness of the velvet vise enveloping him, even in the absence of a barrier, felt like a virgin's. Not that he'd been with any virgins, but this must be how tight, how untried, how uncertain of how to receive a lover one would feel.

And he could only believe the verdict of the body buried in hers. Not only hadn't she been tasted before, her sexual experience was practically nonexistent. And he'd hurt her.

"Samheeni, ya rohi," he panted his agitation. "Forgive me, I should have been more gentle."

"No, no…" she moaned, rigidity draining out of her body. "I never dreamed, *never*…" Her fingers dug into his shoulders, bringing him down to her, forcing him to stroke deeper into her, tearing a hot sharp sound from her depth, a growl from his. He heard exultation mixed with the pain now, and relief flooded him.

She thrashed, never taking her eyes from his, letting him see every sensation ripping through her, her tan brightening with rising pleasure, seeming to glow against the whiteness she lay on, an image the poets of his land, known for their expertise in exaggeration, would have failed to find words for.

"You feel…magnificent…inside me…" she panted, the exhilaration thickening her voice, sending more arousal crashing through his body. "I never knew so much pleasure…existed…"

"Aih, ya rohi, et'mataii…" he rumbled, assurance taking hold. "Take your fill of pleasure."

And he watched in awe as she accepted more of him, arching, offering, abandoned. Her cries rose, her hands bunched in his hair, bringing his lips down to hers to drown them both in another exercise of abandon, her core throbbing around his invasion, pouring a surplus of welcome. She'd reached fever pitch so soon. But so had he. Not that it mattered. He'd succumb now, and would remain ready to pleasure her again, and again.

He withdrew, then plunged, burying himself all the way inside her. And she shattered around him. The feel and sight of her pleasure boiled his seed in his loins. He surged to her womb and her cries intensified, her convulsions reaching new heights, tearing his orgasm from depths he'd never known existed. Overcome, convulsing, he jetted inside her in endless surges, his roars reverberating around the chamber.

He finally felt her melt beneath him, aftershocks jolting through them both. He still throbbed inside her, hard and ready. Still, she wouldn't be again. Not tonight.

He carried her to his bed. The bed he'd spent the past two weeks unable to rest in, imagining her there.

Now she was, lying over him, her eyes drugged with cell-deep satisfaction, humming a wonderful sound, a score of bliss.

She slept. He studied her, all the nuances her features, her expressions, her every breath in sleep revealed, reveling in the unprecedented experience, the unknown intimacy, and was almost sorry when she stirred. Then she wobbled up, her now-dry hair raining over his chest, and gave him a smile that made him feel he could indeed fly under his own power.

"The first moment I saw you..." Her voice was different, awareness-laden, smug. "It was like I turned into a living tuning fork, and your vibe was the frequency that set me off. But no fantasy could have done what you just did to me, what you gave me, justice."

"You gave me as much, and more." Joy burst in her eyes, rained in kisses over him. When the homage reached his heart, it almost rammed out of his ribs for a direct kiss. "But we needed to go through all that we did, to achieve this pinnacle."

She murmured in agreement, undulating in a sinuous dance. "Shehab, take me again, don't make me wait."

"You're sore. You can't take me again."

"I can. I want to feel your weight on me, feel you inside me, dominating me, until I'm finished, complete."

In answer to her pleas, Shehab sprang out of bed, gave her a bedeviling smile as he scooped her up and carried her to the shower. "All mind-blowing pleasure comes to she who waits."

Eight

"I've never heard of strip chess."

At her breathless comment, Shehab lifted a face ablaze with the flames of the fire he was stoking, the majestic sunset and the passion perpetually brewing between them.

They'd dived again today, had had another session in his *hammam,* prepared a meal together, then he'd seen to some business, as he'd been doing for the past three weeks.

Since that day he'd made her his, he'd almost never left her side, had concluded his business on site. She'd been ecstatic yet worried he was succumbing to their magic and neglecting his work. He'd assured her the worst of the crisis was over, that he was now smoothing edges. If he had to leave, he would, but he would take her with him this time. He couldn't be apart from her now. And he never was, never left her side during days and nights spent in the escalating delight of exploring each other.

He'd taught her to fly, in every way as he'd promised, freely admitting that she'd taught him, in turn, how to truly experience and revel in the flight. He said she'd done the same in everything else, made him feel with new senses. And they'd shared everything, from listening to music, to discussing books, movies, world state and business affairs, to preparing meals and tasting food, to sharing jokes and games and silence, to experiencing every nuance of this place, from its skies to its underwater world, from dawn to dawn.

He straightened from the fire, looking straight out of impossible female fantasies, in another of those sumptuous traditional garbs he'd promised he'd wear for her to have the pleasure of seeing him in it, and the far more intense delight of getting him out of it.

This one was more intricate, in gold-embroidered grays and blacks, the open *abaya* billowing around him in the gentle wind like the swirls of a magic spell.

He approached her as she sat under the small shade tent they'd put up, facing the fire. The huge bespoke tent he'd had erected for them earlier was at his back by the lapping waves. His movements echoed the tranquility all around them, deepening his impact, and that of the evocative surroundings.

He came to stand over her, brushed his hand down her cheek. "It does exist, I assure you. You've just led a sheltered life."

She loved his teasing, its wit and gentleness of intention. He was always true to his early words, laughing *with* her and never at her. And loving it when she reciprocated.

She shivered as he came down on his haunches before her. The weather was hot and dry, would become balmy at twilight, cooling gradually as the night deepened, until he'd have her wrapped in the warmth of cashmere and the velvet of his heat. Right now her shudders were emotion-induced. How she *loved* him.

She reached an unsteady hand to the ebony locks that had

escaped the darkness of his headdress, and teased back. "While you've sampled all life has to offer?"

To her alarm his eyes became serious. "Is this what you think? That I led an indiscriminate existence?"

"No. I just meant that you—you've…"

Gentleness reentered his gaze. "It's not unreasonable to think someone with my wealth and power might not have known where to draw the line, might have sought escalating experiments and risks to stimulate his glutted senses. But I assure you, I have no excessive or perverted tendencies, was never idle to get into mischief, and I am extremely fastidious and wary. But not sampling them doesn't mean I don't know all about stripping games. I never saw the appeal, but now, when the game is between us, when it's you…" his gaze dragged down her body, totally obscured in the filmy layers of her own elaborate green-and-gold outfit "…I believe stripping is one of life's most worthwhile activities." He rose, sweeping her up in his arms in one fluid movement, and headed to the bigger tent.

"So this is why you had us dress up in those elaborate costumes? Many layers to take off."

He gave her a scorching smile as he pushed aside the tent flap. And she felt as if a genie might materialize at any moment. Not that he'd know what to offer her. She couldn't wish for more than this. This man, these feelings, this moment.

As for this place, it was enormous, enough to hold a banquet for hundreds, with the tented canvas ceiling undulating from wooden poles, the central one soaring at least fifteen feet, the periphery no less than nine. The ground was leveled and completely covered in a breathtaking array of hand-woven Persian carpets. Everything else, the low couches, the strewn pillows, the tables and urns and lanterns and incense burners, all in a mixture of vibrant colors and burnished brass and copper, was a stunning fusion of many ethnic influences. She could decipher Bedouin, Indian, Ottoman and Moroccan among the blend. And she'd bet that below the authentic decorations lurked all the luxury of ultra-modern amenities.

And in the middle of it all was a twenty-by-twenty-foot chess-board, with pieces made of solid teak and ebony, the tallest, the kings, about four feet tall.

Shehab came to stand in the middle of the chessboard below a hanging brass lantern with Arabian-windows-style glass, its light weaving among the fumes of the sweet-spicy incense, playing over his face. He gave her a playful squeeze. "How about we let the game begin?"

Her head bobbed in a swooning nod on his muscled shoulder.

He set her down on her feet, not giving any sign he'd move away any time soon.

"Your move."

She shivered again at the passion in his voice, moved away reluctantly. She weaved among the pieces, gliding her hands over them, marveling at the perfect smoothness of their polished surfaces, her mind bounding ahead to images of Shehab stripping.

She'd better get her act together, play a killer game.

She moved her pawn forward. He moved his. In five more moves she'd taken his first rook, and looked up at him expectantly.

"Off with your *ghotrah*."

"You have this wrong. The rules are like this. I lose a piece, you strip a piece off of me. You can be as creative, as leisurely as you like in how you do it. And I must stand there and bear it in silence, keeping my hands and every other part of me to myself. Same goes for you, of course. The one who ends up winning has the other at their total disposal for a week."

She rushed to him, her hands stinging with anticipation. "I love the rules of strip chess."

"Actually, those are my rules." He let her reach up and free him of his headdress, groaned and stiffened as she dug her fingers in the luxury of his hair. She urged his head lower so she'd have her fill of massaging his scalp, combing through his hair, twisting locks between her fingers before she finally tugged on them, brought his lips to hers, her tongue gliding over their painstaking chiseling, breaching their seal and dipping into the fount of his taste. He was soon breathing hard, groaning continuously, the hardness she kept pressing against turned to the consistency of rock, his whole body buzzing and quivering with the tension of holding back.

He finally wrenched his inert lips away, staggered back, his heavy-lidded eyes fuming with pent-up frustration. "That everything-off-you stipulation is the most foolish one I've ever made. I almost blew an artery." He shook his head, straightened, moved his bishop and took her knight. "Now I get to pay you back."

She stood riveted, clamoring for whatever he chose to do to her. He dragged her to the ground, went down beside her, took off her sandals, made her discover the one thousand erogenous zones connecting her feet's every bone and inch. When she was whimpering and clawing at him, he withdrew, looked on her condition in satisfaction. "It's a great game, after all."

The game progressed with each getting more creative, inflicting more sensual torment on the other until she was in her lace panties and he in the drawstring pants he had nothing beneath. Then Shehab moved his black queen.

He came behind her, took her with an arm beneath her screaming-for-mercy breasts, murmured in her ear, *"Shah matt."*

"Wha…?"

"Those are the Persian words, what became checkmate. *Shah,* or king, *mat,* or died. You're mine now, to do with as I please."

Her knees buckled at the sheer depth and darkness of his

voice, his passion. "I'm yours anyway, in case you haven't noticed." She ground back into him, felt him hot and hard and huge, throbbing into her back. "But you're wrong."

She twisted out of his arms, stumbled between the huge pieces. "This isn't *shah matt*. This is only Shah, or whatever check was originally called." Her trembling hands moved her queen. "Now it's your king who's *matt*."

He stared at her move for stupefied moments. Then he burst out laughing, peal after peal of guffaws that sent another river of hormones gushing in her system. "*Hada w'Ullah suheeh*—by God, it's true. I didn't even see this coming. I've officially lost my mind, then. Or more accurately, you've stolen it."

"Turnabout is fair play, since you've stolen mine. And now you do as I please."

He spread his arms wide. "Always. Anything. *E'emorini*. Command me."

She stumbled back to him, her prize, heat surging and splashing through her like a relentless fountain, turned and pressed her back into the breadth of his body, stood on tiptoes and squashed her buttocks into his erection. "I want you to take me, just like this, no waiting, no bringing me to orgasm first. I want to come around you, and only around you tonight."

Something reverberated in his chest, wild and voracious as he snatched her up in his arms, rushed to a compartment at the far end of the tent. Behind the waterfall of damask drapes isolating it lay another setting of senses-soaking sensuality, dominated by a huge bed draped in gold and red satin and flanked by mirror-polished brass panels, with a gleaming copper tray table beside it, laden with fruits and delicacies.

He placed her on the bed, on her knees, tore the drawstring off, let his pants pool to the ground as he freed himself. Then he thrust inside her in one stroke.

The blow of sensation as he stretched her beyond her capacity paralyzed her. But it was their reflection in the brass panels, him bending over her back, her kneeling, impaled on his erection, that made her convulse on a sucker-punch orgasm.

"*Aih,* come around me, give it all to me," he growled as she bucked beneath him, screeched and clawed at the satin beneath her fingers. He rode her crest, pressing her down until her face was wetting the satin with tears and sweat, kneading her breasts, her nipples, her mound, spreading her slick core and stroking her everywhere but at the focus of sensations until the pressure inside her rose once more, threatened to implode her.

"I can't...Shehab...can't...too much..."

"You can. You will. Take what you want. Me, unable to wait, driven all the way inside you, your captive, at your mercy. You at mine, taking all of me, like *this*..." He touched her cervix.

Sensations buried her, squeezing wild response from her core, her lungs. "Yes...like *that*...please, don't stop..."

He did, withdrew from her. Before she could cry out, he spread her on her back and plunged inside her again, letting her feel the rawness of the strength that could pulverize men twice her size leashed to become carnality, seduction, cherishing. He undulated his hips, stretching her around his invasion, his eyes leaving her one exposed nerve.

"*E'emorini*—command me. What's your pleasure?"

"Come with me..."

"*Amrek, ya galbi.*" And he rammed inside her. She keened, the pleasures gathering in her core smothering each other around him. She dug her fingernails into his buttocks, wanting him to stab her to the heart. He did, gave her the savagery the epicenter of destruction needed to be unleashed.

She vanished in a moment of whiteout before detonations radiating from his driving manhood razed her, reformed her for the next sweep. Then he joined her in this darkest ecstasy, roaring his completion, his orgasm tapping into hers, boosting its power as his seed splashed into her womb, scorching her and putting out the fire all at once. If not for long, as she knew by now.

A long time later, still hard and throbbing inside her, he rose on his arms. "I trust you're satisfied with my obedience?"

"Any more satisfied and I'd revert to the liquid state."

He moved inside her, drew deep groans from both their throats. "Any more satisfied and I'd burn to ashes. What do you command of me next?"

She was savagely pleasured, boneless yet feeling ambitious. "A swim. Then the barbecue. Then you let *me* take *you*."

He heard the beep. It made no sense for a whole minute. Lying there, wrapped in Farah, still hard inside her, he could feel or think of nothing that originated outside them and their union.

The beep came again. The third time he realized what it was. A message. On the cell phone only three men had access to. His king and his brothers.

"What's beeping?" Farah stirred over him, her internal muscles rippling around his erection.

He thrust deeper into her, unable to contemplate having to leave her. The beep came again. He knew it would keep on doing that until he read the message. Knew they wouldn't send one unless there was something worth disturbing him for.

And he was disturbed. He hated the intrusion into the bliss he was sharing with Farah. Dreaded it even.

"A message. From either my uncle or one of my brothers."

She raised her head off his chest. He groaned as he saw the dreaminess seep from her eyes as alarm inched in. "You think it's something urgent?"

"It must be. Or they wouldn't contact me."

This made her spill off him, and they both lurched, groaned at the pain of separation. "Answer it, then."

With a growl, he succumbed, reached for the infernal phone. The message was from Farooq. **Video conference. Now.** His heart clenched inside his chest. What now?

"Take a shower until I come back. Or sleep a bit. The night is just starting, and I intend to keep you up for most of it."

"Oh, yes, please." She spread herself, inviting, delighting. "And take your time. You'll find me right here, waiting." He took one more kiss from those succulent lips that promised heaven. And they only promised more. "Remember, it's your turn to lie there and let me explore you and pleasure you to my heart's content."

"I'm all yours to do with what you please, *ya hayati*." He plunged for another clinging kiss, then withdrew.

She lay back, watched him with an adoring smile as he stood up, put on drawstring pants and an *abaya,* his eyes devouring her back. Then he gritted his teeth and went to see what the world that existed outside them chose to blight him with.

In his study, he turned on his computer and its three connected widescreen monitors, activated the video conferencing. Farooq and Kamal appeared on two of them.

So, the king still wasn't up to making an appearance. He wondered if his uncle ever would be again. If his own days as crown prince were numbered and his days as king of Judar were hurtling nearer.

Farooq's golden eyes still had that apologetic heaviness they'd been full of since he'd thrown the succession into Shehab's lap. He wanted to tell him to stop feeling uneasy, that instead of saddling him with a burden, he'd done him the favor of his life, allowing him to find Farah, share all this with her, live in anticipation of a lifetime with her. It now turned his stomach to think Farooq might have agreed to marry her. He was certain he would come to feel the same way about her no matter what, and it would have been hell seeing her in his brother's arms, duty wife or not. He couldn't even bear thinking about it.

Before he said any of that, Kamal spoke.

"It's been six weeks, Shehab."

His eyes swung to his brooding brother, met the gaze that seethed with genius and mercilessness. "*Aih*, I miss you, too."

Kamal raised one winged eyebrow, the movement eloquent with abrasive mockery. "You're going soft on us, aren't you?"

Shehab gave his younger brother a considering look even as his comment scraped his tightening nerves. Kamal had always been the one to provoke friction, the one with the harshest opinions, the least compassion. He not only didn't suffer fools, he made *them* suffer. He had followers, but no friends, and but for the presence of Shehab and Farooq in his life, was a total lone wolf. As for enemies, while he had many, no one dared declare the enmity or act on it.

He'd become this rough and ruthless only in the past years, since his stint in the States. He hadn't talked about what had happened there, but he'd come back ready to maul anyone who stepped out of line, like a lion with a festering wound. And he'd remained so, as if all the humanity in him had been extracted.

Shehab finally demanded, "And your definition of *soft?*"

Kamal leaned forward, as if he'd reach through the screen and take up his challenge physically. "Taking six weeks to do what you could have done in six days. *B'haggej'Jaheem*, in six *hours*. You had her on your jet and on the way to your island within that time frame, ready and willing. Why didn't you just—"

Shehab banged his fist on the desk. "Shut *up*, Kamal. If you want to keep those perfect teeth of yours."

Kamal narrowed his wolf's eyes at him, whistled. "You're not *going* soft, you're already there."

"I'll help you knock his teeth out later, Shehab. But we do need to know what's going on."

He turned his eyes to Farooq, heard a squeal in the background. Suddenly all his tension drained. Mennah. Farooq's one-year-old daughter. The smile that surged to his lips came straight from his heart. The little tyke had conquered him on sight. His life had suddenly become so much richer for having the privilege of being her uncle. He couldn't even begin to imagine how he'd feel about a daughter of his own. With Farah…

His eyes searched behind Farooq, hoping to catch a glimpse of the toddler. Farooq understood at once, got up, was back in seconds, his arms filled with the incredible fresh life that, along with her mother, had changed his brother's forever.

"*Ya Ullah,* she gets more beautiful every day." Shehab waved at Mennah, who tried to reach him by pawing the screen, before starting to bang on it in chagrin when she couldn't. He laughed as Farooq pulled her back, telling her in both Arabic and English why she couldn't reach her uncle. Farooq insisted he'd never talk down to her, that she was brilliant and would learn as much as they let her and it was never too soon to start. Shehab happened to agree with his methods. He sighed as Farooq distracted Mennah. "Where's Carmen? And how is she?"

At the mention of his wife, Farooq's eyes kindled with the heat of love and lust, the warmth of pride and trust. "She's taking a shower. And she's magnificent."

"She's out of the shower. And look who's talking."

Kamal gave a rough exhalation of impatience as Carmen appeared behind Farooq, taking both him and her daughter in an exuberant hug before looking at Shehab. She did look well. She was a lovely woman, but now she truly glowed with the overpowering beauty only absolute love and happiness could generate. He was happy that Farooq, who'd always carried the weight of the world on his shoulders, had found the one woman who'd love him as endlessly and unconditionally as Carmen loved him. No wonder Farooq had so easily given up the throne for her.

He watched Farooq and Carmen share a kiss that for all its lightness and brevity told volumes about the depth of their relationship, in and out of bed. He knew the signs now. What a fleeting look, even the least gesture or nongesture could convey. For he shared it all with Farah.

Carmen took Mennah from Farooq, smiled at him and Kamal. "It's great to see you again even if on a screen. Now, say bye, Mennah. Your father and uncles have important stuff to discuss."

Mennah let out a loud, protesting *"aab."*

"She's trying to say my name!" Shehab exclaimed.

"Of course." Farooq grinned his elation, before turning to Carmen to share their special smile. "She's a prodigy."

Shehab laughed at Mennah's continuing efforts to throw herself at the screen. "I promise I will soon come to you and we can play catch-you all day long."

As soon as Carmen and Mennah disappeared, Kamal grated, "It's so heartwarming to see you both enjoying your family life when our whole region is on the brink of widespread civil war."

Farooq glared at Kamal's screen, then exhaled and turned to Shehab. "It's true, regretfully. The Aal Shalaans are getting restless again. They're demanding proof that King Atef's daughter will marry you, that we aren't only pacifying them until we find a way to cheat them out of having their lineage introduced into our royal family. They gave us two more weeks, threatening extreme action afterward. I don't know what's been going on on your end, and I don't want to know. But you now need to give us an answer. Will she marry you, or won't she?"

Shehab closed his eyes. So the time had come. He had to ask her. And she was indeed ripe to say yes to anything he asked.

She'd been that for weeks now. But he'd felt that, as soon as he asked her, he'd be counting down to the moment she'd find out the truth. He hadn't been able to face the possibilities.

So he'd shut out the world, had taken all he could with her while he could.

Now the world had come crashing back on him and he had to brace himself for its weight, its reality. Its inescapability.

Feeling bile fill him to his eyes, he ground out, "She will marry me."

Nine

He reentered his quarters, theirs now, covering the long distance to their bed slowly, to savor the image she made, naked and tangled in the sheets, one breast jutting out, nipple still erect, just because he was there, existed, her thighs pressed together on the ache of satiation and the renewed need he knew must be gathering in her body as it was in his.

He stood over her and she opened her eyes, the look of total desire and delight there skewering through him as she held up her arms, spreading herself for his ownership.

He surrendered, filled her arms with a pained groan. She rained kisses over his face, his neck, his shoulders and he shuddered, drew back. The hungry, playful look in her eyes gradually turned uncertain, then anxious.

"What is it, darling?" She came up on one elbow, a quiver that thrummed in his heart permeating her voice. "Is something wrong with your family?"

He squeezed her shoulders, forgetting anything but what had churned inside him like slow poison since he'd laid eyes on her, the one thing he had no answer for. The one thing he needed answered. *Now.* "Only one thing is wrong. One thing I need to know. When you leave here, will you go back to your lover?"

She fell back on the bed as if he'd backhanded her.

"H-how did…?" She gulped, squeezed her eyes shut, her color rising until she almost glowed in the dimness. At last she opened her stricken eyes. "W-was that what this phone call was about? You've investigated me?"

"Did I need to investigate you, Farah? After all the things we shared, you couldn't have told me yourself?"

She scrambled up to her knees, her eyes filling, with tears and beseeching. "I should have, but I couldn't. I was so thankful you hadn't heard the rumors…"

"Rumors? Are you telling me Bill Hanson isn't your lover?"

"Oh, God, no. He's the only one of Dad's acquaintances who stood beside us when Dad died and all our assets were lost. He offered to give us whatever we needed to regain them. But my mother admitted her lack of business acumen was what led to our losing Dad's fortune in the first place, and that she'd only lose whatever Bill gave us again. I was too young to take over and soon realized that I wasn't cut out to be the CEO of a multinational corporation. So I asked him for a job instead. He offered me one at a huge salary, and I worked my tail off to earn every cent. He soon promoted me to his personal advisor and analyst. When I accused him of being charitable again, he insisted I was the best person for the job, having been taught by Dad, who was the best, not to mention that he trusted me implicitly, something he couldn't buy with all his money.

"The rumors started the day he promoted me almost two and a half years ago, and Bill asked me to let people think they were true, said it was a mutually beneficial arrangement. I wanted to keep suitors away, and he wanted revenge on his wife, who'd left him for a man their youngest son's age. I was content with the arrangement until I met you, and I was so happy you hadn't heard about it as I just wasn't up to explaining, was even afraid you might not believe me."

She fell silent, out of breath, her eyes seeking his reaction anxiously. He doubted he had any outward reaction. He felt as if he'd turned to stone.

After he'd become certain she hadn't been sexually active, his mind had taken off on ugly tangents to explain how a woman could manipulate a man like Hanson without using her body.

But he'd dismissed each explanation as impossible. Not her. Not Farah. And now this. This demolished every doubt. Made her a total innocent. Made his deception infinitely worse.

For he believed her. Without question. She was only telling him what his every instinct had been telling him from the first moment. She didn't have one exploitative cell in her body.

But there was one thing. He grabbed at it to yank him out of the mire of realizations and guilt. "Why didn't you want suitors, a woman of your youth and beauty?"

"*Suitors* was the term Bill used. Mine is *predators.* I've had them circling since Dad died, first for my inheritance and then since I became Bill's right hand, because of my position."

"That's why you…?" He choked on his question, memories bombarding him.

"Why I accused you of having some sort of agenda the night we met? Yeah, my insecurity reared its ugly head. I was so stupid, it even crossed my mind that you might have something in common with those petty men who wanted a piece of Bill."

"But surely you realize that you, alone, without any other incentive, are enough to drive men wild?"

She gave him an incredulous look. "Yeah, right."

"How can you even doubt it? Don't you see what you do to me? What you did to me since that first look?"

"I think it's a miracle, that you want me as much as I want you. But before you, I didn't care if there were men who might want me for myself. I never wanted a lover again, after my one experience left me convinced I was incapable of enjoying sex."

One experience. So she'd been as inexperienced as he'd felt. Her first real intimacies, her first pleasures, her first abandon had been in his arms.

But the elation of this confirmation was dampened by everything else. The expanding knowledge of how much his initial preconceptions—no matter that they'd been backed up by photographic evidence—had caused him to misjudge her. They'd polluted his thoughts and feelings, kept him resisting logic and the evidence of his own senses and intruded upon the precious moments with her, moments he hadn't fully appreciated, believing what he had about her. And now this. And he had to know the rest, everything. Struggling with a dozen reactions, he said, "Tell me about this experience that led you to believe such a ludicrous thing about yourself."

She looked as if she'd rather dig a hole and hide.

Just as he was about to tell her she shouldn't recount it if it upset her at all, she squared her shoulders, gave him such an adorable look of embarrassment and determination.

"I was nineteen and I was still trying to cope with losing Dad, with being the strong one for my mother's sake. Dan was one of Dad's executives and he kept working on convincing me that I needed someone, that that someone was him. His research of me was so thorough he knew what to do, what to say, to project the image of a soulmate for the embarrassingly green girl I was. But then, as a shrewd businessman, he would have sunk that much time and effort into far less than the half-billion-dollar deal I still was at the time. He was ready to do anything to land me. Then he did, and it was—" she winced, the perfection of her lightly tanned skin turning coppery with embarrassment "—horrible. It wasn't even painful, for he was—uh…" She put two fingers about four inches apart, turning positively red. "Anyway, it was just awkward and gross. And he told me it was OK, that some women aren't capable of enjoying sex, but he would keep trying to—to…"

"Cure you?" he spat.

She winced at his sharpness, nodded. "Something like that. Seemed he counted on me being so ashamed of my shortcomings, I would let him steer me whichever way he wanted. But you know me. I'm incapable of hiding what I feel. So I said, if I couldn't enjoy it, didn't want it, why bother? He tried to humor me for a long time, but his act started to crack. Seemed that when all the work he'd done wasn't paying off, his endurance started to give. Then one day I blurted out, why not just be friends? And he erupted. Just like a volcano. Kept spewing for an hour, honest. Who would want to be my friend? He'd only endured my inexperience and my odious character for the money, which he thought he deserved, not a brainless idiot like me. I was amazed. I'd aggravated him to the point where he threw away half a billion dollars rather than put up with me. Then, when said money was lost, he even called me, gloating over his lucky escape and over the fact that I was now not only a cold bitch but a penniless one, too."

Shehab glowered at his hands, feeling his every nerve charging up with murderous intent.

But was he any better than this man? Hadn't he done the same to her? Manipulated her to an end unconnected with her? As she'd felt from day one?

No. *His* cause was just. And he'd started his own manipulation under false impressions about her, the worst. And he'd pleasured her, would die before he hurt her in any way. While that man, who'd deceived her, scarred her for life…

He rose, stood on the bed, looked down on her. "I'll find that scum. Then I'll send him on a one-way trip to hell."

She blinked in alarm, then gave a nervous giggle. "Oh, Shehab, he's not worth one drop of this magnificent machismo. Save it all for me."

"You're not buying him mercy like you did the paparazzi," he bellowed. "The man who made you think being hounded by them was preferable to being exposed to his species, the man who convinced you you had something lacking, when you only have extra endowments, the least of which was the sense to feel repulsed by his dirty soul's touch, when there's no woman who has more sensitivity, or is more capable of being ignited and pleasured than you. He robbed you of your innocence when he didn't even want it, when he reviled that incomparable gift. And he'll pay, slowly, for all his crimes."

She gave a huge sob, launched herself at his legs, hugged them. "Oh, Shehab, if you want to avenge me, you just did. More fully and fantastically than you can ever know. Just forget him, or you'll make me scared to tell you anything from now on."

He looked down on her, grappling with aggression, with the raging emotions at seeing her like this, at his feet, the cover pooling on her thighs and exposing the sweep of her graceful back and flared hips in a pose out of his deepest erotic fantasies. He felt his turmoil leveling as his aching eyes glided over the luxurious waterfall of her sun-kissed hair cascading between his rigid thighs, her lips almost buried in his erection.

He took all he could then snapped, sank to his knees before her, hauled her to him, mingled her with his limbs and lips.

He came up from the endless kiss, looked down at her as she

lay in his arms, her eyes drugged, her trembling hands pushing his *abaya* off, exposing him to her hunger.

She started talking again as she pushed him to his back, to start the exploration she'd claimed a right to, one of the events he now lived for. "But this guy was right about one thing. I did experiment with physical intimacy after him…" He stiffened, and she soothed him. "I didn't go beyond kisses, with good-looking men I found nice enough, agendas and all. I'd decided to go in with my eyes open and have fun. I thought if the kisses went well, I'd go further." He started to growl and she dipped her tongue into his navel. "I hated the first's scent and taste. The second's voice, his breathing, the noises he made in his throat made me want to slap him. With the third, when I found myself thinking when I can get this over with so I can go back to that donut I was eating, I knew Dan was right about me being unable to enjoy physical intimacy." He came off the bed when she buried her face in his erection, inhaled him, moaning long in enjoyment. Then she raised her head and looked him straight in the eyes. And her eyes. *Ya Ullah,* her eyes.

This was Farah, letting him see into the very depths of her heart and soul. Then she told him.

"But I realize now I can't feel physical passion without an emotional one. And that's why you'll always be the only one to ignite and pleasure me. Because I love you."

Everything ceased. To matter. Ceased, period.

Because I love you.

He stared at her, paralyzed under the onslaught of every contradictory emotion in existence. She loved him. *Loved him.*

And she was taking his hand, her trembling lips burying in its spasticity, her eyes glittering with so many emotions, he felt inundated. "I loved you at first sight, and I've been falling deeper every moment since."

Was this how necrosis struck in someone's heart? With emotions that actually generated damaging heat, like a laser? Could he have been blessed by so much, the love of this incomparable woman, her total trust…when he deserved none of it?

But no. He deserved it. For she'd seen through the thin layer of manipulation to the emotions that had blossomed toward her unchecked, unstoppable from the first, every spark of it true. That was what had made her fall in love with him. She'd been reciprocating his feelings.

And though he felt he deserved to lose her in atonement for how he'd led her on, how he still couldn't confess everything, since it wasn't only his life or fate in the balance, he had to reach out and take all she offered. And she was offering her all. And he needed it all to live, to exist. He would throw his own need at her feet.

He slipped off the bed, pulled her to its edge until he had her sitting up, then kneeled between her legs. He wanted to pour it all out. But he couldn't. He was overcome. She had overcome him. He lowered his head to her knee, reiterating her name raggedly, as if in deepest prayer.

She cried out, tried to pull his head up, her fingers trembling in his hair. He put his on top of hers, pressed them to his head, showed her he wanted to be cradled in her lap, needed to be held to her heart, surrounded by her generosity, blessed by her love.

And his magnanimous Farah complied, hugging and hugging him, spilling hot love and tears all over his face and hands.

"Please—" she hiccupped "—don't make me sorry I told you. Don't feel as if you owe me anything. I know how honorable you are, and I'd die if I made you feel bad, or compromised. I knew what I was doing, and I never expected anything in return. I'm just happy I'm normal, that I found you, a man who deserves my total trust and love. When it ends, I'll go on knowing I experienced true fulfillment. That for once I had what my name proclaims me to be. Joy. You gave me that, and I'll always cherish the memory of our times together."

He stared up at her, struck at the horror of what he'd inflicted on her. She might have subconsciously felt his emotions, but she'd been unable to believe they existed. And she still hadn't protected herself at all. She'd given him all of herself, trusted him, expecting nothing, believing she'd have nothing of him in return, convincing herself the morsels he'd given her so far would be enough.

He surged, clamped his lips over hers, unable to bear one more word. "*B'Ellahi, ya habibati, er'ruhmuh*…have mercy, my love. *Ahebbek, ya farah hayati, aabodek,* I love you, joy of my life, I worship you. It's I who loved you on sight, who wanted everything to be perfection for you, wanted to give you time to know me as I prayed you might come to feel a fraction of what I feel for you. You own my heart, by right of being the first to ever wake it. You own my body and life, by right of offering yours for them. And now you own my soul by right of giving me your essence in all selflessness. But you say you don't expect anything of me. Does this mean you don't want it? Won't you take it, when I offer it? Everything that I am? Will you not make me complete, give life reason and texture and purpose? Will you not marry me?"

Farah had gone still with his first words, her eyes, those emerald heavens like pools in an earthquake, their waters welling, shaking in place. When his heart emptied of blood and wouldn't fill again, silencing him, she gasped as if she'd been underwater, was coming up for a life-saving breath. Then the pools of her eyes turned to rivers, and her face shuddered out of control with jubilation and disbelief. And finally, belief.

And he was in her arms, crushed to her breasts, surrounded by her delirium and joy and the absoluteness of her love.

And she sobbed it all to him, the one thing he craved to hear, her happiness as she consented. "Yes, yes…yes, yes, I'll be your wife, I'll be with you always…" She withdrew, her eyes wide with wonder and love so fierce it was painful. "Oh, God, you really love me."

He reared up, spread her on the bed, came over her. "*Ana aashagek*—I…I…there's no word for it. *Esh'g* is a concept that has no equivalent in English, more selfless than love, carnal as fiercest lust and as reverent as worship and as impossible to shake. I always thought it part of the innate hyperbole of my culture. But it isn't, it's the one thing that approximates how I feel for you, about you, with you. *Aasahagek. Enti mashoogati.* What I feel, and what you are to me."

She melted beneath him, nerveless, overwhelmed. "It's too much…oh, darling, too much…"

He consumed her gasps, drained her tears. "Nothing will ever be too much for you, everything I have or do or feel or am is yours. *Enti rohi, hayati*…my soul and life…"

She arched beneath him, in a fever, opening her legs around him, clamping them high on his back. "Please, my love, I can't take anymore…just take me when I know it's in love this time. Love me, let me love you.…"

He stroked into her, invaded her, surrendered, and that was all it took to bring them to ecstasy. This time, when he jetted his seed into her womb, he roared his love. And he was freed, free, completed, complete.

"Of course I know it's been six weeks…" Farah bit her lip as she put the phone away from her ear at the tirade that exploded on the other end. "Bill, will you calm down?" She raised her voice into the mouthpiece before venturing to put the receiver to her ear again. "I *will* do the analysis today, promise." She paused, and Shehab couldn't hold back anymore, walked to her, swept her up in his arms, took her to the couch, sat down with her on his lap, smoothed her, soothed her. She gave him a look that was a cross between gratitude at his solicitude and aggravation at Bill's fit. Then she finally exhaled. "OK, OK, Bill. Don't give yourself another coronary. I'll come back. As soon as I can arrange it."

She ended the call, looked up at him, apologetic.

He only growled. "You don't have to take orders from him anymore. As my wife you can buy him out a dozen times over."

A look of bliss came over her face the moment he said *wife*. She melted in his arms, memories of their tempestuous, magical night written in her expression, fusing his insides with love and longing for a continuation.

She came up from another surrender to their deepening bond, gasping, and chiding him. "First of all, I'm not marrying you for access to your limitless funds and power. Second, this isn't about money. Bill is sort of the only friend I have, and he needs me."

He grappled with the need to tell her to let Bill go to hell. "I accept and understand that." And he did. He knew he was enough for her, but if others enriched her life in any way, struck an extra ray of happiness in her heart, he'd cherish them, too, do everything so she'd have them in her life. But… "He won't raise his voice to you again, though, or he'll suffer."

"Oh, he's just all bark. With me, at least. In fact, he's sort of comforting. Dad used to be the same, and it's sort of nostalgic having a father figure with the same audio effects."

"You keep stopping me from defending you, with all this misguided compassion." She started to protest and he only kissed her. "And though it aggravates me, since I can't let my wrath loose on all who've ever given you a moment's discomfort, it's one of the endless things I love about you."

"Oh, do you think you can arrange for me to have a list of those, in writing?" He gave her a hard, long kiss, swearing he'd arrange for her to have the moon if she only wished for it. She pulled back, panting. "So you'll arrange for me to go back to L.A.?"

Shehab's heart convulsed with trepidation. After the enchantment of the past six weeks, confessing their love had catapulted them to a higher level, one that kept getting higher with each moment of knowledge of each other's love. And he dreaded the least change. But how could he deny her?

He couldn't. He'd always give her anything before she even wished for it. "You think I'd send you back alone?"

She jumped in his arms, whooping in delight. "You'll come with me?"

"To the ends of the earth, to hell and back, or even if there was no return ticket. So what's a tiny skip to L.A.?"

The tiny, twenty-hour skip, reprising their memorable flight from L.A. to his island, was the reverse of everything that had taken place then. While then they'd spent it talking, and strictly outside the bedroom, this time they headed there the moment they boarded and didn't come up for breath all through the flight.

But through the sensual delirium and emotional overload, Shehab felt anxiety and the need to pour out everything he was withholding from her, everything that was eating at him.

Yet he'd look at her, see and feel her adoration and bliss, and have his purpose defeated again and again. How could he cloud this perfection by bringing up the charade that had started it all? How could he cause her pain and disillusion if only for moments, before she believed she'd long stopped being an instrument for securing the throne of Judar?

It was only as he finally watched her walking into her workplace, turning every two steps to wave at him, that he knew.

He couldn't put it off any longer.

As soon as he saw her again, he would divulge his identity, confess the whole truth, beg her forgiveness for the deception that had ceased to be one almost from the start.

And his magnanimous Farah would forgive him.

She turned around one more time before she disappeared behind the mirrored glass of the skyscraper's entrance, blew him a kiss. He caught it, pressed it in both his hands to his lips, before taking it to his heart, where it took it and soared.

Yes. He'd confess, and she'd forgive and forget.

Then their lives would truly begin.

Ten

Farah floated all the way up to Bill's office. She smiled left and right at all the people she knew or didn't know. She even skipped as she passed Bill's sedate personal assistant. She didn't wait for anyone to announce her arrival, just sailed through his door.

She found him at his desk, his elbows resting on it, his head between his hands.

And all the jubilation that had been bubbling over inside her since Shehab had kneeled at her feet stilled. Besides Shehab, Bill was the strongest person she'd ever known. No matter what blows he sustained, personally or professionally, he weathered them all without any outward indication of pain or weakness. Now he looked spent, defeated.

She rushed over to him, and he raised a bruised gaze. "Your lover brought you back promptly, I see. Do you know who he is?"

She started at his harshness. So he knew why she'd taken the sabbatical. Figured. Bill would find out anything he put his mind to. But why was he glaring at her? Was he worried she might have divulged vital information about him during pillow talk? She had to put his mind to rest at once.

"Yes, of course I do, but…"

His harsh sigh cut across her qualification. "Lord, I wasn't ready for this, even though I knew you were bound to change your mind about sleeping with men. And who better than this man, eh? Sleeping with him serves so many purposes."

Farah's discomfort metamorphosed gradually into confusion. Was something wrong with Bill? He was making no sense.

And he went on, making less and less sense. "Perhaps the world is telling me something, that I should admit it was me who pushed Stella away. But if I've had enough, got over the rage and heartache, maybe it's time to see if she's learned her lesson, too." He glared at her again, his eyes blazing blue in his florid face. "But why didn't *you* confide in me? Though I'm floored that, for once in your personal life, you've made one move that's good business—in this case, the best business—I would have understood. Hell, I would have given you pointers."

"OK, I'm calling your doctor. You're talking gibberish."

Bill sighed. "Who thought you'd have the sense to test-drive Judar's crown prince before consenting to marry him? These royal Middle Eastern marriages are forever, after all. But from your blind expression as you walked in, seems you found Shehab Aal Masood's sexual prowess…satisfying, to say the least."

The world stopped. Became a vacuum.

It seemed hours later when it restarted with a screech and air tore into lungs that had collapsed with shock.

"You think Shehab is…" She coughed the hysterical giggle of someone who'd just escaped being hit by a bus. "But I can see how. The crown prince's name is Shehab, too, huh? Guess it must be a popular name. Likening their sons to the grandeur and destruction of meteors must appeal to those desert lords. But Shehab's last name is Aal Ajman. He's the tycoon who—"

"I know exactly who he is. The tycoon who seemed to come out of nowhere three months ago. Aal Ajman is his mother's family. I bet he didn't think I'd investigate that when he created his alter ego…" He stopped, rose slowly to his feet, a tide of rage advancing over his face as everything seemed to fall in place in his mind. At the same moment it did in hers. "But I wasn't his target with the deception, neither was the business world at large. *You* were. You refused to marry him, so he decided to con you…" He stopped again, horror replacing rage on his face. Or was it only a reflection of the one on hers?

But there was no horror inside her. Realizations too atrocious to register, to take in, bombarded her, like the meteors Shehab was named for. And like a meteor shower, they left only annihilation in their wake. The nothingness of wreckage.

Shehab. He was not the man she thought she knew to the farthest reaches of intimacy. He was the prince her newfound father had said she must marry. The one she'd refused to even hear about. She'd thought she had a choice. But she'd had none. He'd hunted her down to have her rescind her refusal, relinquish her will, surrender her heart and soul, her life. Things he had no use for. He'd been talking about himself when he'd described how Dan had manipulated her, taken from her, when he'd reviled the gift she'd made of herself.

She'd felt his exploitation that first night, too. She'd just been too ignorant to suspect its truth, then too eager to disbelieve her senses and believe his coaxing.

How he must have hated to perform for her benefit, how he must have loathed every second in her company, must be seething with impatience until he could discard the pawn he'd been forced to cater to, to make her obey his tribal laws.

She suddenly heard her voice, the distorted sound of a zombie. "I want a favor, Bill. I want to use your helicopter."

Bill's eyes narrowed. "He's waiting downstairs for you. You don't want to see him."

"No. Never again."

He exhaled heavily, nodded, reached for his intercom. His hand froze over the button. "You'll let me know where you are." She gave a sluggish nod. He persisted. "And you won't hurt yourself…in any way."

She looked at him out of someone else's dry-as-stone eyes and wondered how he'd even worry.

How could she hurt a self that had already been destroyed?

Shehab gave in, stormed into the skyscraper after Farah.

She'd been inside for three hours. And for the past hour, her cell phone had rung with no answer.

Inside, he met with evasions until he resorted to threats. Only then did he discover she'd left the building by helicopter.

He stormed outside again, telling himself to calm down.

She must have left on the urgent business her boss had called her all the way back there to deal with. She'd call as soon as she was done. She probably hadn't thought he'd wait for her to get off work. And she probably hadn't heard the phone over the helicopter's din.

Nothing he told himself worked. So he did what every self-respecting, madly in love man in pursuit of the woman who held his fate in her hands to confess his crimes and beg forgiveness would have done. He tracked down her phone's GPS signal.

Even with the endless resources at his fingertips, it took four hours to locate her, and then fly to her location. A bungalow hotel in Orange County.

After a good look at Shehab's diplomatic passport and a short explanation about the situation, a duly awed desk clerk told him where to find Farah, even gave him an extra card key.

Shehab walked there, his heart's pounding escalating as he caught her scent on the wind. He could have followed it, and her vibes, to her exact location without being told where she was. Doubts intensified with each step, too.

This didn't look like a place where any business of Hanson's could be conducted. So why had she come here? Why had she not called him in so long?

Before he slotted the key card in, something made him knock on the door instead. After long moments of silence, steps neared, slow, almost dragging. Then the door opened.

A stranger stood across the threshold.

A stranger who looked exactly like Farah.

So it's true, Farah thought.

She'd opened the door and found Shehab there. And she hadn't felt a thing. Not shock, not surprise, not anger, not pain. Nothing. It was over.

"Habibati…" he groaned as he surged forward, surrounding her, his impossibly handsome face, the face that hid all his cruelty and deceitfulness, contorting on another array of those expressions so uncannily simulating emotions. "I almost drove myself insane when you didn't answer your phone. Why are you here? Is this where Bill sent you? What for?" When she didn't answer, only slipped from his arms to close the door, turned to look at him out of some other entity's eyes, he moved closer like a panther careful not to let its prey realize it would be a meal in seconds. *"Hayati,* what's wrong?"

He still didn't realize. Or he was still trying to bluff his way out of it? He probably thought he could. She was too stupid to live, after all. She'd proved it for six long weeks.

But something terrible was happening. The sight of him, his scent, the feel of him, the very idea of him was seeping through the layers of numbness. The total anesthesia was lifting. And damage began to spread through her, expanding, taking shape, endless in scope, in details, the enormity of his betrayal, of her gullibility.

Crazed with pain. She now knew what that meant, felt like. She could feel everything that made her a person, that formed her mind, disintegrate as each memory of the past six weeks regurgitated to the surface like oozing acid, until her brain was a mangled mess.

And he took her in his arms again, shuddered as she filled them. As if he cared if she lived or died.

She visualized an escape. A version of reality where she was the woman the rumors painted her to be. The woman who wouldn't only survive this, but who would walk away laughing. Invincible like him, playing her roles to gain her ends. Ending each without feeling or remorse. Heartless.

But she was heartless now, too. He'd hacked out her heart.

She pushed out of his arms. "I want to thank you."

His gaze wavered. He couldn't read her for the first time. And he was worried. "What for, *ya habibati?*"

Habibati. My love. *His* love. When she was his nothing. Just an instrument, a means to an end. Every word a lie. Every touch and smile and moment—worse than a lie. A cold-blooded, abhorrent role he'd had to play, to get her to succumb to her role in his kingdom's politics. She was a chess piece he'd maneuvered with inhuman skill, premeditation and indifference.

And she couldn't let him go on laughing viciously at her expense, knowing he'd made her his grateful, worshipping fool.

She channeled his female counterpart, heard herself murmuring coldly, "You did what everyone before you failed to do. You're the only one I had a liaison with who Bill knew was a real threat. But then you're the first crown prince I've ever been with.

Of course, I knew. I went along because you wanted to play it that way, and I wanted to play, too. But it really made him panic. He called me back to offer marriage at last."

Before Shehab doubled over in shock, he realized.

Farah had found out who he was, was teaching him a lesson.

Now she'd slap him for keeping his identity from her, rant and rave, then end up laughing at his deserved horror. And he'd sweep her in his arms and let her have whatever revenge she saw fit. Then much, much later, he'd show her how he'd take anything from her, but there were certain things she should never joke about, or use in his chastisement. One thing. Her love for him.

But she didn't slap him, didn't rant, didn't laugh, just looked at him with those unfamiliar eyes, spoke again in that unfeeling tone. "It's been fun while it lasted. You're a great host and an OK lover. I'm sure you didn't mean your marriage offer, but even if you did, Bill is by far the better proposition. You're too...demanding, you understand."

He couldn't breathe. He wouldn't until she yelled at him, or until she made a face and stuck out her tongue, as he loved to see her do. But she did neither.

She passed him, opened the door. "Bill is very sensitive about you right now, and I have to humor him until he writes up those prenups. Maybe after everything is settled I can see you again. If I don't hook up with someone else meanwhile, that is."

Everything he'd heard about her. The rumors as she'd called them. She was admitting to them all. And she wasn't joking.

"Of course, if we do hook up again, you'll have to excuse me when I drop the wide-eyed, adoring idiot act. I strained to keep it going and won't be trying it again any time soon."

Stop. *Stop.* The roar bloodied his throat, even when it went unbellowed. But she didn't stop.

"I would have invited you in for goodbye sex, but Bill's joining me in an hour, and you don't do quickies, so..." She made a dismissive gesture, showing him the door.

He couldn't have moved if his life depended on it. An avalanche had buried him, made up of all the moments since they'd met. Every one twisted around, grinning hideously, showing him its true macabre face. He'd deceived her about his intentions for the best of reasons. She'd deceived him about her nature, seamlessly, for the basest ones.

The woman he worshipped didn't even exist.

But he couldn't stagger to his knees and bleed to death now. It didn't matter if she was a perverted soul who thrived on entrapping men only to destroy them. It didn't matter that she'd pulverized his heart and soul. Those were the man's. The crown prince of Judar didn't need them to fulfill his role as future king. And he'd make her fulfill hers—as future queen.

He took the door from her, closed it with a calm that only losing everything can bestow. "So you think you can just send me on my way. Interesting. More interesting is that you seem to think any of the last six weeks was actually for you. A woman's ego is boundless, especially when enough flimsy men give her the impression she is irresistible. I would have preferred to do this my way, the painless way, but since you think I'll let you merrily go on to your petty agendas, I will have to apply pressure. It's up to you how much I do apply. You can come with me now, without further persuasion on my part, and spare yourself the unpleasantness, or I can make you, and your senile lover, live to regret it. *Then* you'll do what I want, anyway."

Farah almost smiled. How easy it had been to make him take off the mask. Bare his true face. The soulless sheikh who used and abused people to his ends.

With the morbid fascination of someone mortally wounded and wondering how her murderer would release her from the pain, what the killing blow would be, she cocked her head at him.

"You're drunk on your power, aren't you? How would you do any of that? We're in America now, not your island, or in your kingdom."

The smile he gave her would have been scary, if she could feel a thing. "Can I give you a list? How about starting with grinding Hanson into the ground, until he's filing for bankruptcy? If I show him how I'll do it, and how he could stop it, he'll throw you aside in a blink. Then I won't leave you anywhere else to turn and you'll come crawling to me. And I'll take you, marry you, a repulsive duty for my kingdom's sake. I only endured your so-called inexperience and your odious character to obtain my end. The highest end. Retaining the throne of Judar, and with it the whole region's peace."

And it came. The confirmation. The end of hope that maybe anything, one hour, one time with her, had been for her, had been real. It was Dan all over again. He'd even used his words.

But Dan she hadn't loved beyond self-preservation, beyond sanity. His animosity and disgust hadn't mattered to her. Shehab's finished her.

And she was pushing past him. Running and running.

She didn't get far. In a minute he had her cornered between his men and his approach. And like prey that knew there was no point in struggling, she stood there, let him catch her.

He took her to his limo, his eyes those of the stranger he was, his real emotions fueling his gaze, pitilessness, aversion. She sat huddled against her door all the way back to his jet.

As soon as they were in the air, she turned lifeless eyes on him. "So you're kidnapping me for real this time."

He made a disgusted sound. "I'm taking you to your father.

Fate has it that you're the daughter of a great king, and the salvation of two kingdoms. I have to look beyond your shortcomings and at what good you'll do by simply existing."

"What's this stuff you keep talking about? Retaining the throne, the whole region's peace, the salvation of two kingdoms?"

"King Atef told you all about it. Spare me the pretense."

"I'm not pretending. I've talked to King Atef maybe a dozen times. The first few times I was still reeling after my Mom dropped the bomb that he was my father. I—I really liked him, but I was afraid I might be desperate for another father figure.

"He was so eager to know me, seemed so happy to have found me, and I started to open up. But I still felt like a yo-yo. One minute I'd get excited about finding him, the next I'd feel guilty, as if I were betraying Dad's memory. Then he came to meet me and told me I had to leave my life behind to marry a prince I'd never met as part of a political pact. And I knew that his friendliness had all been another setup. He wasn't happy to know me, had only been saying whatever would get me to go along with his plans. I couldn't listen to a word he said after that, told him to just leave me alone."

"And so, thinking your feelings were the only thing to consider, you refused to marry me. That's why all this happened."

She stared at him, another layer of misery suffocating her.

He glowered back. "But since you'll regrettably be Zohayd's princess and Judar's future queen, you should know how things stand. I'll pretend your question indicated interest, or at least curiosity." He paused, as if expecting her to comment. When she kept staring at him, desolation deepening, he exhaled.

"The Aal Masoods have sat on the throne of Judar uncontested since they brought all feuding tribes under their rule and founded the kingdom six hundred years ago. But our king, King Zaher, has no male heirs. And then, both his brothers, one of them my father, died, leaving only his nephews to rise to the succession. With the direct line of succession broken for the first time in six hundred years, the Aal Shalaans, the second-most influential tribe in Judar, felt it was time for their turn on the throne, and their demand was accompanied by threats of an uprising that would end Judar's reigning peace.

"Offering them settlements didn't work, and options dwindled to a forceful solution—a solution that would lead to civil war. A war the Aal Masoods will do anything to prevent. Even if it means losing our throne, which would still mean tearing Judar apart. Then Judar's neighbor, Zohayd, was dragged into the crisis, for another branch of the Aal Shalaans form the ruling house there."

"So King Atef is an Aal Shalaan?"

"As you are. You didn't even know his full name?"

"I—I didn't want to know anything more. I didn't know—I didn't think—I…" Her defense stifled under the mercilessness of his gaze, which before had been sympathetic, empathic. But he was done acting. She choked out, "So what happened after that?"

It was a long moment before he continued his account, his voice grating her raw. "The Zohaydan Aal Shalaans pressured King Atef to support their tribesmen's rise to Judar's throne. But he wouldn't support such madness. The Aal Masoods are his biggest allies and the reason behind Zohayd's prosperity, not to mention that losing our throne would destabilize the whole region. He was willing to side with us in a war against anyone, kinsmen or not. But that would have plunged Zohayd into civil war, too.

"After intensive negotiations, the Aal Shalaans in both kingdoms decreed that the only peaceful solution was for the Aal Masoods' future king to marry the daughter of their most pure-blooded patriarch so that their blood may enter our royal house.

Things calmed down as disputes lengthened over which patriarch in their extensive tribe had the purest Aal Shalaan blood, with Farooq, my older brother, then Judar's crown prince, poised to marry his daughter. But that patriarch was determined to be King Atef himself, who didn't have a daughter.

"It was then we all realized we'd fallen into a trap, realized who'd been behind the conspiracy. It was my cousin Tareq, the outcast would-be crown prince. He stirred old hatreds, cornered us until we had no way out but to fight for the throne. Or to let it go. Either way, Judar and Zohayd would be destroyed in civil wars that would drag the whole region into chaos. He plotted a perfect revenge on the royal house that had cast him out, and the kingdom that was its biggest ally. Then a miracle happened. King Atef discovered he had a daughter from an American lover. *You.*" His eyes blazed down her face and body, razed her. "And a pact was struck between the two kingdoms, thwarting the conspiracy, appeasing all involved. But my brother Farooq loved his wife so much he couldn't contemplate taking another wife, no matter the cause. So he stepped down. Now it's my responsibility to save the throne of Judar."

And there was silence. For what had to be hours.

So he had a legitimate cause for destroying her. She was what the military liked to call collateral damage. But then, what did she matter in something of this scope? The fate of a whole region hung in the balance. And he'd been forced to do whatever was necessary to bring the stupid goose who'd unwittingly been about to tip everything into hell in line, to fit into the critical slot haphazard fate had placed her in.

"King Atef…m-my father should have insisted on explaining…"

His teeth clapped together before scraping a sound that made her nausea surge. "He must have conveyed the exigency of the crisis. But as you confess, you didn't listen. Why would the fate of two kingdoms you can't find on a map matter to you?"

She raised those eyes that belonged to someone else, beyond hurt or pain now, praying she'd remain in that dead zone forever. "I'll marry you."

Something terrible flared in his eyes. She would have cringed if she'd had a life to fear for.

He finally grated, "And of course that noble decision has nothing to do with knowing that it's your only option now that you've lost every bet you made."

She shrugged. "You won. What else do you want?"

He lowered his eyes, his spectacular eyebrows drawing together as if on a spasm of pain. Then his gaze shot up, slammed into her, hostile and enraged. "I want *you*."

"No, you don't."

Shehab heard Farah's deadened dismissal and wondered if this was how men broke, under the weight of agony and disillusion so vast, they just buckled.

He'd already known they'd come to the point when he had to force her to marry him, by any means necessary. There was no other option left. This was far bigger than either of them.

But she'd consented, without further pressure. As if she were consenting to an amputation.

Memories of her first consent, the ecstasy of it, gored his mind. To know she would marry him now as a capitulation, a compromise, was crippling.

But what made this beyond his ability to withstand was what he'd confessed. To her. To himself.

He damned himself for feeling anything—*everything*—for her after she'd smashed his heart, his faith, but there was no escape for him. There never would be.

But if she'd made him her prisoner, he'd make her his.

"Yes, Farah. I *want* you."

Some life entered her gaze, agitation, alarm. "But you said…"

He exploded to his feet, stormed to her, plucked her out of her seat and into his arms. "I don't care what I said. It doesn't matter what either of us intended or planned. The one reality here remains this…" His mouth crashed down on hers and she convulsed in his arms, cried out. He took advantage, thrust inside her, his tongue driving with unchecked emotions.

He strode to the bedroom in which they'd lost themselves in each other's arms only hours ago. A lifetime ago. When they'd been different people. He placed her on the bed and came down on top of her. She cried out again, pushed at him.

He stilled at her struggle, slid off her. He'd never force her, not even the woman she'd revealed herself to be. But he'd force her to acknowledge one thing. "You want me, too. I know when a woman feels pleasure at my touch, but you—in my arms, you disintegrated in ecstasy. You're shaking with needing me inside you, assuaging the ache, giving you the release only I can bring you. Don't even try to deny it, because I know. And if this is all we can have, then we'll have it. All of it."

He held her eyes, demanding her concession, her confession.

And she gave it. With her lashes hiding her expression she dragged his mouth back to hers, scorched him in a blast of hunger as her hands trembled at his belt. He growled in relief, in agony, tore at her clothes. He had her naked, only shredded his shirt open, freed himself, settled his chest over her breasts, rubbed her to a frenzy as she clamped her thighs around him in silent supplication for him to invade her, to merge them.

Unable to stand one more heartbeat outside her heat, her hunger, he rammed inside her.

And right there, buried inside her, knowing that the next thrust would hurtle them both over the edge, he stilled. Reared up. Looked down into her eyes, saw it. The soul that was right, that was perfect, for him, come to complete him, discovered to show him what life held of possibility, to fulfill the promise that had remained unrealized until she was there.

Then she moved, taking him as he took her, her eyes never leaving his. And the dam of pain and anger and disillusion shattered, and every beautiful, overpowering thing he felt for her flooded him. Images of a child with emerald eyes and hundred-color hair deluged him as he jetted inside her, feeling he'd poured his lifeforce into her, causing her paroxysm to spike. Ecstasy rocked them, locked them in a closed circuit until it seemed they might not survive the heights of pleasure, the depths of agony.

When he felt as if his heart would never restart, the excruciating release finally relinquished its merciless grip, let it beat again. Then she let go of his eyes, the deadness back. And the madness lifted, left him groping for breath.

"All those things you said were fabrications." His choking words were not a question. They were him, realizing the enormity of the mistake he'd made. "*Ya Ullah,* why did you say them?"

She moved, making it clear she wanted to end their merging. He groaned at the pain of separation, had no choice but to watch her get out of bed like a malfunctioning automaton, go to the wardrobe he'd filled with clothes tailor-made for her, pulled on an emerald summer dress that had made her eyes iridescent when she'd first tried it on. Her eyes were muddy now, vacant.

"I'm just beginning to realize the full implications of you being the crown prince of one of the most powerful oil states in the world. You probably hold the power of life and death over your people. You want it over me."

He rose from the bed, shuddered at the lifelessness of her voice as he did up his pants, approached her. "I don't…"

She cut across his protest, her voice becoming an almost inaudible rasp. "You don't think it enough to have me where you want me, a pawn in your political game and an eager body in your bed, proving your irresistibility. You want to wring me of the last drop of dignity to placate yours."

"*B'Ellahi,* Farah, stop. This isn't what I…"

"You want to know why I said what I did? Can I give you a list?" She echoed his earlier taunting. "How about a reaction to finding out I was means to an end all along? Or wanting to walk away from the worst degradation of my life with the illusion of being on equal ground? Or needing to make you show your true face, so it would be superimposed on that of the man I loved, erasing it from my heart and mind so I can go on living?"

"*Atawassal elaiki,* I beg you, *ya habibati,* let me…"

"I beg *you* to stop. Your plans worked, you got what you wanted out of me, in every way. So go do your duty and take your pleasure with whomever you want for real, for herself, let her provide the ego strokes you need and *leave me alone.*"

He tried to reach for her. "I can't…"

She staggered away. "Not until I give you an heir? Is that why you'll keep having sex with me? What if I told you—"

"You *must* listen to me. What I said, how I've behaved in the past hours, I was only lashing out after all those ugly things you said. *Ya Ullah,* you made them sound so convincing, the blast of shock blew away my memory, my knowledge of you. But even before you explained, I remembered, each moment—"

"I remembered each moment, too." She cut across his desperate words, and he looked on in horror as she seemed to fragment before his eyes. "I'm remembering now, each look, each touch, each word I said to you, each sensation as I listened to you, as I felt you touch me with your eyes and hands and lips, cover me, move inside me. And I play it back and super-impose the truth over the illusion. I see your real feelings and thoughts as you watched me squirm in longing and pleasure and hope, as I fell flat on my face in love with you. I see you as you hid behind your shield of indifference, gauging when to poke me, how to make me beg, pant, and humiliate myself more and more."

He surged, blind, out of his mind with agony, with the need to absorb hers, clutched her into a frantic embrace. She struggled wildly, tore herself away, quaking on sobs so hard he feared they were tearing her insides apart.

"God…the way you strung me along, the way I looked up to you, thought you unique, a man who cares about a woman's feelings, not just her body, who cares about *me*. And all the time you could hold back because I was nothing to you, because you felt *nothing*. All the time you watched me making a fool of myself, lapping up the crumbs you kept dropping, yelping in gratitude. How pathetic did I seem to you, craving your appreciation, dis-believing my senses and believing in your every lie, bursting into flame without you even trying, writhing in pleasure at your merest touch, begging for more? How ridiculous did you find my inse-curities and gullibility and readiness to die for you? How much did you snicker the moment my back was turned? How hard did you laugh when you were alone? *How hard, Shehab?*"

Her accusations, the realization of the extent of the damage he'd inflicted on her, paralyzed him. For the first time in his life he felt powerless, helpless. How could he undo a wrong of this magnitude? Heal wounds this deep?

He fell to his knees before her, like a detonated building, struck, mute, her tears raining on him, burning away his soul.

He finally heard a thick, unrecognizable voice choking his defense, his plea for leniency. "I did manipulate you, but only because I believed the lies I'd been told about you. By the time I knew they were only that, I couldn't risk your reaction, so I kept on deceiving you about my identity, but that was the extent of my deception. The magic we shared was real, from the first moment. *Ana aashagek.* I never lied about my feelings for you. I was going to confess everything, today, but *ya Ullah,* I left it too late."

Her tears turned off abruptly, the nothingness creeping back on her face. "It's really my fault. I was reckless and self-destructive and I got what's coming to me."

"No, *b'Ellahi,* you will believe me, believe that I care about nothing anymore but you, and restoring your heart and faith in yourself, in me. I will spend my life…"

She raised a steady hand. "Just…don't. It doesn't matter if your pawn is intact or glued together. I will serve my purpose."

The rest of the journey was consumed by his frantic efforts to reach her. But it seemed the most vital mechanism inside her, her soul, was damaged beyond repair. She'd opened herself, given of herself so fully to him, and the blow had shattered her.

Shehab felt desperation becoming resignation, that she'd never trust him, or feel the same boundless emotions for him again. And he'd die without her trust. Without her love.

But he didn't matter now, or ever. Only that he restored her. Only that she would be whole once more. But he no longer knew how he could do that. If he could ever do it.

All the way to the royal palace, she pulverized his heart all over again when she didn't resist him when he reached for her, stroked and kissed and swore his love over and over.

And he knew. She'd succumb to him, to her duty, to the hold he had on her senses, and she'd die slowly. She was dying now.

And it came to him. What he must do. What he would do.

He'd let her go. Completely.

* * *

They were entering King Atef's court when he finally decided how to phrase his resolution, started to voice it only for her gasp to silence him.

His gaze followed her shock, found King Atef standing between two women—his sister and a tall, slim, blond woman. Anna Beaumont, Farah's mother. But it wasn't surprise at her presence that he felt, but trepidation at the expression on their faces.

As they approached, Anna looked at Farah with reddened eyes, mouthed a soundless, "I'm sorry."

Farah wobbled at his side, and he hugged her to him fiercely, glaring at King Atef. He understood nothing, but he'd give his life not to have her wounded again.

The king had eyes only for Farah as he came forward, the pain on his face portending devastating news.

Then he delivered it. "Farah…I can't tell you how sorry I am, but it falls to me to divulge a most upsetting fact to you. As much as I rejoiced in finding you, now it crushes my heart to lose you. You are not my daughter."

Eleven

Farah stared at the man she'd seen only once before.

His face, a desert warrior's, one who'd weathered the brutality of nature and the tests of power and position, had been carved in her memory, demanding to be acknowledged as her father's.

He was telling her he wasn't her father after all.

His eyes were heavy with regret as he elaborated. "Evidence of your paternity was required to introduce you into the royal family, to complete the pact with Judar. We obtained a hair sample from your residence. DNA results were conclusive."

Conclusive. Just as everything she'd been too upset or hurt to fully register, let alone acknowledge, became.

In spite of her shock and resistance, with her mother so distant and the vacuum of Francois Beaumont's loss still gaping inside her, she'd been increasingly comforted thinking the king was her father, right up until he'd sprung the arranged marriage on her. And in spite of her pain and humiliation, she'd known she'd have no life without Shehab, had yearned to marry him for whatever reason, had hoped he'd meant even a fraction of his protestations. That one day, what had started as a duty for him might turn out to be a real and satisfying relationship.

Now she had no father.

And Shehab wasn't duty-bound to marry her.

It was over.

She closed her eyes and begged silently for the pain to just finish her.

But something like a butchered bird flapped inside her chest. She tried to still its struggle, to no avail.

It kept screeching that maybe now that the king had no daughter, the two kingdoms would find another way to forge their alliance, and Shehab would be with her for a while longer…

"But my real daughter has been found."

She lurched as the king's words impaled the wild hope, killing it on the spot. And the king was going on, every word twisting the knife further.

"It turned out her mother—your mother—had given *her* up for adoption." His burdened gaze turned to Farah's mother, who was looking as if she was about to faint. "Then she married Francois Beaumont, adopted you, a two-year-old daughter, as a substitute for the daughter she couldn't forgive herself for giving up."

He then looked at the squirming woman by his side who was clearly his blood. "My sister was the one who adopted Aliyah, raised her as my niece among her family even if not in her rightful place. During the latest upheavals, she finally came forward, and another DNA test has just proven her allegation." King Atef's gaze settled on Farah, more pained than ever. "I regret all this more than I can say, but Aliyah is my daughter. And Shehab must now marry her at once."

Shehab. His embrace had been surrounding her with his strength and presence all along. Only the consecutive blows had distracted her from homing in on his reactions to the shocking developments.

But she'd never seen into his heart as she'd been so certain, so giddily, ecstatically, stupidly certain, she had.

He kept insisting he'd never deceived her about his emotions, that the cruelties he'd uttered had been the only outright lies he'd ever told her.

But he took his duty to marry for the throne very seriously. He could have been making the best of this mess, placating the woman who'd be his wife, to smooth the course of the marriage Bill had described as forever.

Now the name of the woman he had to marry had changed.

As long as he fulfilled his duty, would he even care which woman he took to his bed? Would it matter whose body cried out for his, who lived to love him?

She lurched again, and his arms fell away, the only things that had been keeping her together during the maelstrom that had uprooted her existence, left her without identity, origin or direction. And she got her answer.

No, he wouldn't care. He'd never cared. None of it had ever been for her. She'd been King Atef's daughter to him. Now that she wasn't, Farah no longer mattered.

He'd already let her go. She'd already ceased to exist.

Had she ever existed at all?

She swayed, sinking into the mercy of numbness, her eyes focused on the king. The man who *wasn't* her father. Neither was Francois Beaumont. She had no father…

"You have nothing to apologize for," she whispered. "I should be the one apologizing for the misconception. My mother should be, my mother who…who isn't even my mother…"

The king was the one who surged toward her, his hand around her mother's arm, bringing her nearer with him. "No, my daughter…" She jerked, stumbled back. He stopped, his eyes gentling, realizing the pain the word *daughter* had inflicted on her. "You must not blame your mother. You have to understand how it all happened. I loved your mother deeply, but I had to give her up, could never be with her, even after she discovered her pregnancy. I was unable to acknowledge the child, and with so many demands tearing me apart at the time, I told her to get rid of it. I regretted it even as I said it, and never stopped regretting it, but I did think she'd terminated her pregnancy. I forced myself not to seek news of her for long years.

"Then I had a heart attack, and, faced with my mortality, what really mattered became clear. I acted on a gut instinct that always told me I had another child, searched for your mother, found out she had a daughter the exact age my child would have been, and didn't doubt for a second you might not be mine. It was only when the final steps of admitting you into the royal family necessitated proof of your parentage that I sought it. After the negative results, investigations ensued, uncovering your adoption. It seemed we were back to square one, where the crisis is concerned, until my sister Bahiyah confessed the truth and I had your mother flown here to get the complete story."

Her wavering gaze turned from him to her mother.

Lies. It had all been lies. From the beginning. Everything she'd ever believed about her life. With her mother and father. With Shehab. Even now, what she was being told—all the so-called facts turning everything that she'd believed about her identity, her history, her very life upside down all over again—could turn out to be more lies.

Her mother's face, open for the first time with blatant emotion, streaming with tears, begged her leniency.

She had none to give as the dam of deadness shattered, swamping her with agony and disillusionment.

"How could you do this to me? Why did you let me, and him, believe I was his daughter? You regretted adopting me, wanted to foist me on someone else, didn't you? Why? I was never a burden to you, I only wanted you to love me, or at least not to resent me. I never understood why you did. I thought I'd found the answer, thought I reminded you of the man you loved and lost. But you only resented me because I wasn't yours all along…"

The king tried to intervene again, but her mother clamped a hand on his forearm, stopping him, staggered to Farah, clutched her shoulders in rabidly strong hands. "*No,* Farah. I *never* resented you. It was always the opposite. I wanted to adopt you from the first day I saw you, only you, out of a hundred children. But they refused me, a single woman who'd just a year earlier given up her own daughter for adoption. Then God sent me Francois, and he moved heaven and earth so we could adopt you. He agreed that you were ours, should never be told otherwise. You know how he loved you. You were his world. But I was sick, Farah. And he stood by me, hid the fact that I was in therapy or you would have been taken away from us."

"Therapy? You were in *therapy?* And you never told me?"

"I couldn't tell you. It was about you, and I didn't want you to feel responsible or guilty. But I had these overpowering emotions for you, unreasonable fears of losing you, and Francois soon made me see I was stifling you. You wouldn't remember, since I've been in therapy since you were six. Ever since then I've been constantly struggling to pull back."

Farah let out a laugh full of bitterness. "You succeeded too well. I always thought I was such a disappointment, that you could barely stand me, especially after Dad died."

Anna shook her head, her hair sticking to her wet face. "No, no, darling, no. I was going crazy after Francois died, wanted to cling to you with all my strength. And I knew you'd let me, would bear all my need and weight and never complain. I knew you'd let me rule your life and time and drain you. And I couldn't do that to you. I wanted you to live *your* life."

"So you let me live it alone. Is that what you thought best for me?"

"Don't, darling, please. Please try to understand how hard it was, the anxiety attacks, the need to hound your every step. There was no middle ground for me. It was either suffocate you or let you go."

"So you let me go. And now I don't have a mother at all…"

"Don't say that, darling, please. I *am* your mother."

And Farah screamed. "*No, you're not.* If you cared anything for me you wouldn't have done this to me. Don't you know what you did? You let them think I was this vital missing piece in their grand scheme and they sent Shehab after me. I was content with my life, solitary as it was, expecting nothing special to happen to me. Then he came, and I actually dared dream of more, was actually happy—blissfully happy—for a few weeks. And now it's all over."

Arms tried to pull her in their embrace, infinitely strong and gentle, shaking, but she was blind, mad, struggled like a cornered animal, tore away until a cold surface stopped her momentum. She found herself slumped against a marble column, heard nothing but the horrible sound of her own weeping.

Anna's sobbing voice rose into her consciousness. "When I k-kept silent about your identity, I thought I was giving you a new father to love, who w-would love you, and a life of undreamed of privilege. I didn't know where or who my biological daughter was. I wanted you to have the birthright she should have had, and I thought she'd never have now. I wanted to help Atef and his kingdom. I never thought for a second that I could harm you, and that I have and this much—oh, God, my darling…f-forgive me. For everything…"

Farah staggered around to face her mother. "Have you met your real daughter?"

Anna shook her head, reached out imploring hands.

"When you do, never tell me about her. I—I can't have even a mental picture of her…"

Sobs overwhelmed her again as she imagined Shehab, his magnificent body open to the worship of the faceless woman, a woman fit to marry a king, a princess born, favored by all, the instrument of peace and prosperity, his equal in beauty and refinement, sharing his background and culture, versed in all the nuances she'd never known, and in the arts of seducing and servicing her man.

And he'd take his pleasure inside her, spill his seed where it would take root, as it…

"I can't bear it." Hands came over her at her cry, each imprint a brand. She cringed at each, screamed, "Don't *touch* me."

The hands withdrew, and the world swam, everything swelling and distorting, inside and out.

At last she heard herself rasp, "Who are my real parents? Do you even know them?"

Anna only hiccupped a great sob, shook her head again.

And Farah wailed, "Oh, God…*I'm nobody's.*"

Shehab had to stop Farah. Had to stem her agony before it killed them both.

But before he could dash to contain her, she was careening to the door, her beloved face shuddering, her eyes gushing tears that looked as if they were blood-tinged.

He lunged with the surge of fright, caught her arms, examined her tears frantically, his fingers dipping in them, rubbing at their texture, almost sagged with relief to find it all in his abused mind.

She shook her head and tried to squirm out of his hold, refusing to meet his eyes. "I'm s-sorry…for all the time and effort you wasted on me. But you now h-have the woman who'll solve your problem a-and you'll never hear from m-me again…"

He knelt down before her again, collapsed. "*Er-ruhmuh ya Farah*…mercy. If you don't want to kill me, even though I deserve whatever you do to me, I beg you, stop. Stop tormenting yourself. None of this, none of us, especially not me, is worth one of your precious tears."

She stared down at him, her tears running faster instead as a shaking hand flailed down his cheek before whipping away as if he'd burned her. She looked at it in stupefaction. It was wet.

And he realized it—he was weeping, too. He'd shed tears only at his mother's deathbed. Not only for her loss, but for what she'd endured before death had spared her the suffering. His father's death had been so sudden, yet somehow expected. Shehab hadn't been able to feel real grief when he'd felt his father had gotten his heart's desire, rushing after his wife.

Now he wept, for the grief he'd caused the woman who'd become the one thing he wanted from life. The woman who deserved to be cherished by all, who now felt that she never had or would ever have anyone.

He'd set her straight, once and forever. "It's not true you're nobody's. Even if it were, it wouldn't matter. You're mine. As I'm yours."

Everything stopped. Her tears, her breaths. His heartbeats. But he knew he wouldn't convince her that easily. He must…

"You must stop this at once, Shehab." That was King Atef, agitated now, severity entering his voice. "I will do everything in my power to compensate Farah, but you have a duty."

Shehab only took Farah around her hips, hugged her as she swayed, supporting her as he turned his head to the king. "Yes, I have a duty…" He turned his face back up to her. "To the woman I love. I beg you, *ya farah galbi,* joy of my heart, marry me."

Farah jerked in his hold, gasped, her tears flowing again, splashing all over his upturned face, mixing with his.

He hugged her more fiercely, buried his face in her bosom, begged, "Marry me, let me live my life filling yours with security and fulfillment." He raised his eyes, seeking evidence of her starting appeasement and healing. "I want only you, no agendas, just need, just love, for you, and nothing but you."

Her hands swept over his head, his face, as disbelief warred with creeping elation and hesitant belief on her expressive face.

He hurried the latter. "Yes, believe me and in me again, I beg you, *ya maboodati.* It's true, every word and touch and pledge were true, and all for you."

She still shook her head. "But you can't…I'm not…"

"And I'm *ecstatic* that you're not. As long as you were the king's daughter, you would always have thought marrying you served my original purpose. I was about to let you go, would have moved heaven and earth to have peace without the need for our marriage, would have begged to remain your lover, to become your husband only when you believed that I wanted you for yourself. But now it's better than what I didn't dare imagine. Now you're only Farah. *Mashoogati.* You'll be sure that every minute from now till the end of my life is for you, and nothing and no one but you."

"Enough, Shehab," King Atef roared. "Don't be cruel, don't go promising the child what you will not be able to fulfill. As Judar's future king…"

"As Judar's future king I have to pay the price of not pledging myself to Farah." Shehab cut across the king's righteous wrath, rose to his feet, cleaving her to his side. "And since that's an impossibility, then I gladly abdicate."

The world had stood still so many times since she'd laid eyes on Shehab. This time it streaked, as if to skip his declaration, unable to actually record it.

But nothing could lessen its impact. Or stop it from storming through her.

He wanted to abdicate. For her.

He'd been telling her the truth. He felt the same.

He felt the same.

He hugged her off the ground, burying his face in her neck where his still-wet face singed her skin with the concept and reality of his tears. *His tears.*

And she couldn't bear it, wouldn't have it, that she'd be the reason for his pain, his loss, for discord.

She clung to him, took his face in her hands. "If you're doing this so I'll believe you, you don't need to. I do believe you. I believe you, my love. But you can't walk away from your duty."

"I can..." he turned his lips to one of her hands, then the other "...and I will." He suddenly threw back his head and laughed, the most marvelous sight and sound to ever occur on the planet. "Do you know who I love almost as much as I love you at this moment? Kamal. I'm ecstatic to have him for a younger brother. I now understand how relieved Farooq was to have me next in line, to pass the throne and its attached wife to."

"You mean...? But you...and he couldn't be..." Her stuttering came to a halt before she burst out. "I can't let you do this, not for me. You may regret giving up so much, and I can't—"

"It's giving *you* up that would have been giving up my very life. Kamal will be the future king. He is probably more suited for the role than I am. And he's unattached, so marrying Aliyah should be no problem for him. I and Farooq will still be princes, second and third in line, and we'll go on as before, ensuring Judar's greatness and the region's stability."

At her continuing objections he placed a finger on her lips. "I'll never regret my decision, *ya mashoogati.* My only regret is and will remain ever hurting you, losing your faith, if even temporarily. It almost killed me, to see you in such pain, pain I inflicted, to feel you breaking up inside, drifting away from me where I felt I may never reach you again. You're the one I was born to love, the one my heart was made to beat for. You awakened me to a world I never dreamed existed, you saved me, *ya farah rohi,* joy of my soul, and you own me."

She threw herself at him, murmuring incoherencies, covering him in kisses and reciprocations. And he stood, taking it all, showered, taken, blessed.

Then it was time to let in the outside world. Only because he believed she needed it to complete her healing.

He turned to the others who'd been watching them all along.

"This will work out for the best," he said to the troubled but clearly resigned king. "Kamal is a far better statesman than I am."

The king gave a harsh bark. "You're letting your brother, the region's most uncontainable force, enter a union with my nie…my daughter, the region's most volatile entity, and you're promising me the best results? If there's anyone who can make the Aal Shalaans rue their machinations and the Aal Masoods regret succumbing to them, it's those two."

Shehab laughed, dropped a kiss on Farah's alarmed mouth. "Maybe they'll be exactly what the region needs."

"Don't you mean what it deserves?" the king scoffed, before approaching, bringing with him the still-weeping Anna and his highly moved sister.

"My daughter, forgive me for opposing Shehab's pledges, but I was unaware of the depth of your involvement. I have to say I was alarmed when I saw this would lead to settling on the last Aal Masood brother…" He winced, as if settling on the devil would have been preferable in his opinion. "But now I'm only grateful Shehab has a spare heir, even if it is Kamal, so he can give you what you deserve, the best this life has to offer. In the time I thought of you as my daughter, I truly came to care for you. I hope now you'll be my daughter's *selfah*—sister-in-law— and by virtue of sharing a mother, her sister, that I'll be in your heart as you are in mine."

Farah gave a strangled sound and catapulted from Shehab's hold to throw herself at King Atef, hugging him around the waist and sobbing, "I would have loved having you for a father. I k-know you'll be in my heart…" She raised hesitant eyes to his. "And in my life?"

The stunned king groaned, hugged her back. "*B'Ellahi,* it would be a privilege and an honor, *ya bnayti.*"

At this point, Shehab feared Anna would collapse, or worse. He turned to her. "And I hope you'll feel as enthusiastic about having me in yours, *ya sayedati.*"

The woman's color became dangerous, her eyes never leaving Farah's face as she stuttered. "Yes…yes, of course…"

He tugged at Farah, who'd stepped away from the king, murmured in her ear, for her ears only, "Make peace with the mother who loved you so much, she didn't know how to love you. Guide her, *ya habibati,* like you guided me, in how to love, then take all the love that's due to you."

The flare of love and gratitude in her eyes was so pure, it was more bittersweet torment, his Farah's specialty.

Then without further recriminations his magnanimous Farah swept her mother into her embrace. "I always wanted to make you proud and happy, Mom. I love you. You shouldn't have struggled alone—you should have let me help you. And I will, from now on." Anna burst into another weeping jag, and Farah soothed her, kissed her cheeks, hugged her more securely. "Don't feel bad, Mom. It's over. As for all the things I said, look how wrong I was. If not for you keeping silent, I wouldn't have found Shehab, wouldn't be happier than a human being has a right to be now. And I didn't mean it, about Aliyah—uh, or I did only because I thought Shehab would marry her, not because she's your real daughter. I hope she lets you, and me, be part of her life. I'd love nothing more than to have a sister."

"Aliyah most certainly would love nothing more, too." That was Bahiyah, smiling tentatively now. "She always wanted a sibling, namely a sister."

"This means you'll be my aunt." Farah threw her arms around the woman, to Bahiyah's delighted surprise. "I always wanted an aunt, too."

The gathering soon moved to the king's family room, where Shehab watched Farah winning over everyone around. And though he wanted nothing more than to sweep her away to be alone together again, he let them have as much as they wanted of her and she of them.

Hours later, the king had left and only Anna remained, getting acquainted with him and getting reacquainted with Farah. It was only when Shehab felt the mother/daughter relationship was on the path to true balance that he finally decided to bring the warm gathering to an end.

He bent to kiss his future mother-in-law's cheek. "I would have insisted that you come with us now, but I know you are King Atef's guest and have another daughter to forge a relationship with. When you're ready to come to us, our home is yours."

He bent to Farah, who was looking at him with her heart emblazoned on her face, and swept her up in his arms. "Now, pardon me. I need to take my bride-to-be home."

An hour later, aboard his jet in their bedroom, Farah turned in his arms and whispered, "Is all this happening? I have you? And I will have my mother at last? And maybe a whole new family, too?"

He smoothed his hand lovingly down her back. "It's all happening, the least that you deserve, *ya malekat galbi*."

"You will translate every word in Arabic from now on. I want to speak it as soon as I can."

He chuckled. "I promised to teach you everything you want. *Malekat galbi* means 'ruler of my heart.'"

She bit her lip. "Speaking of rulers…there'll soon be another who'll rule both our lives. I suspected it, did a test in that bungalow before you arrived, and…and I…I'm pregnant."

He froze. Her words stumbled over each other in alarm. "W-we never used protection, and it was reckless of me, but I always thought I'd end up adopting or having a child without a father, since I wasn't going to have a man in my life. But I-I loved you, knew I'd never love again, and I thought i-if I got pregnant with your baby I'd have a part of you forever…"

He crushed his mouth over hers, then withdrew to give her one shake. "You…you…" He had no words. For the first time in his life. But he had to find them.

He sat up, reeling, raking his hands in his hair. "You had better watch what keeps spilling from these lips, from this mind, or you may end up married to a madman with a very short life expectancy." He turned, snatched her onto his lap, hiding her in his embrace as if afraid she'd disappear. "You would have walked away carrying my child, sacrificing yourself? What did I tell you about sacrifices? You *will* give me your pledge never to sacrifice anything again."

"Having your child alone would have been no sacrifice but

my very own miracle. Now she or he remains so, besides having you. And I certainly won't pledge such a thing. I'd sacrifice anything for you, so you'd better learn to live with that. Just like I have to learn to live with the huge sacrifice you made for me." He started to rumble that it had been no sacrifice, that he was only waiting for the chance to give to her as much as she'd given him, but she silenced him with her next words. "And I want to have at least one more baby. Uh…if everything goes OK with this one…and, uh…if it's OK with you…that is…"

He swung her around, above him, overcome. "There's nothing I want or hope for more than to fill my world with outspoken, enslaving replicas of you. Every time we made love, I did wish for a child made of our love and pleasure. But know that I'd be happy with one, or with none. I'm happy just having you…"

It wasn't until they were landing in Judar that emotion relinquished its hold enough for him to speak again.

"Welcome to your new home, *ya ameerati*…my princess."

She smiled in expectation, sat up, twisted to look outside the window. Wonder crept over her features. "This looks like another planet."

He chuckled, trailed kisses up her back. "And I'll give you a wedding from another time, another realm. A *One Thousand and One Nights* reproduction the likes of which the kingdom has never seen."

She turned, alarm firing her eyes. "But you saw how I handled attending a sophisticated party and wearing an elaborate gown. I'd die if I embarrassed you in front of the whole world."

"Uh, about that…" And he confessed his setup.

After he'd borne her punishment in delight, she looked up from her revenge, flushed and excited, before her face fell again. "Still…those events can take endless planning and we'd probably see nothing of each other for weeks. Didn't you pledge every *minute* to me?" Her flush deepened as she hastened to add, "Not that I want you tied to my side or anything, but think of all the minutes we'd waste chasing our tails during the hectic preparations."

"We're both in luck, since Farooq's wife, Carmen, is apparently an event-planner fairy. I bet she'll wave her magic wand and free all those precious minutes for us. I promised you everything, *ya mashoogati*. And you'll have it all."

"I already have it all...uh, how do you say *habibati* and *mashoogati*, for a man?"

He kissed one hand. *"Habibi."* Then the other. *"Mashoogi."*

And she kissed both of his, tears of joy filling her eyes. "I already have it all, *ya habibi*. I have you, *ya mashoogi*."

He squeezed his eyes shut. "And how you do."

She feathered them open, attempting a teasing smile. "How?"

"I'll show you how. You have fifty years?"

She sighed, kissed his neck. "For starters."

"You're too generous, *ya farah rohi*. And you're too lenient. You should have drawn out my torment."

She gave his jaw a sharp nip, giggled at his indrawn breath of pained pleasure. "You're into S and M?"

"I want you to get satisfaction."

"Oh, I did. I do. How I do."

"Show me."

She showed him. And as he drowned in her love and pleasure and magnanimity, in *her,* he knew beyond a doubt. She would always show him. She was the reason he'd been made how he was, so he'd love her, be hers.

He thanked God again for the crisis that had brought them together. For all the things that had conspired to give them the gift of each other.

And now, the miracle of their love had been given new life...

* * * * *

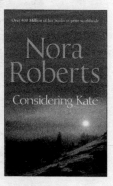

The World of Mills & Boon®

There's a Mills & Boon® series that's perfect for you. We publish ten series and with new titles every month, you never have to wait long for your favourite to come along.

Blaze.

Scorching hot, sexy reads

By Request

Relive the romance with the best of the best

Cherish™

Romance to melt the heart every time

Desire™

Passionate and dramatic love stories